The Middle Ground

Shon A. Butler

McClain Printing Company
Parsons, WV
www.mcclainprinting.com
2019

International Standard Book Number 0-87012-903-1
Library of Congress Control Number 2019905507
Printed in the United States of America

Dedication

To my Christina whom I love deeply. I cannot accomplish what I do without you.

To my JasiBug,
I am not a perfect man but will always strive to be your perfect "DaDa"

To the other children. I love you deeply, Alyssa, Kelsie, Alecsis, Erica and Eli.
From turmoil comes love. Christina and I love you very much.

To my parents for turning me lose on the woods
and waters and not being helicopter parents.

To my good friend Steve Smith who has inspired me to dig deep into
West Virginia's history and artifacts. He showed me the thrills of blacksmithing,
building things with my own hands and uncovering why I always got the sense
of being "home" when I was standing on Big Sandy Creek
in Rogers Fork, Roane County, West Virginia.

To Papal and Grandma Butler, I wish you were here to celebrate this book
with me and the history I have uncovered.
You all touched my life unlike any other influences.

About the Cover Artist

DAVE HASLER
"Art of the American Frontier"

I grew up in the Genesee Valley of rural western NY state where my roots were planted in the history and heritage of the area. It has greatly influenced my artwork. From the Seneca to the Sullivan Campaign.... from Fort Niagara to colonial scouts...the American Frontier has always fascinated me and is a source of much of my artwork.

I have shown my art all across our country and have been the featured artist on the cover of the NMLRA magazine Muzzle Blasts many times. I live in rural western NY state in the small village of Leicester with my wife Janet. We have two grown children and one granddaughter. After retiring from 32 years as an art instructor I now devote the majority of my time to drawing and painting subject matter from the American Frontier.

Please contact me for original artwork and limited edition prints at: dhasler16@gmail.com; Text: 585-991-8478
You can also find Dave's art on Facebook at Dave Hasler Art.

iv

About the Chapter Art Artist

I wanted to introduce you the reader to the artwork of my good friend Josh Simons of Upshur County, West Virginia. Josh is a native West Virginian, he loves spending time in nature with his family, hunting and camping. Josh is a forester for the West Virginia Division of Forestry and is an amazing public servant that gives of himself to improve our forest lands in our great state. Josh also has another skill that he is working on that I am quite jealous of. He has started down the path of making custom longrifles. He truly is an all around artist and good friend and I want to thank him for the contributuions to this book.

Shon A. Butler

Introduction

There is a strip of land between the Allegheny Front in the east to the Ohio River in the West. From Pittsburgh in the north to Kentucky in the south. This strip of land is the Middle Ground.

Long considered a hunting area by several Native American tribes and owned by none, it was a land filled with elk, bison and deer. The big predators flourished here, bears, wolves and panthers. Furbearers were everywhere. Hunting, trapping and fishing was a way of life.

The forests were full of Chestnut. That mighty tree that the white man wiped out with his careless activity of introducing nonnative species. The most ghetto chestnut that flowers in June and never is frost bitten therefore producing a crop of the extremely tasty and high protein nut without fail. All other tree species growing to magnificent sizes. The amazing plant ginseng carpeting the forest floor all through the middle ground. The streams full of brook trout as one writer put it, "a foot and a quarter long and four inches across right behind the gills. Turtles, catfish, sturgeon, paddlefish and a great array of giant and edible fish. It was no wonder the Native American tribes fought to maintain their way of life. Moneto had given then everything they would ever need.

The French came and lived and intermingled with the Natives which made them tolerable. The English, Scotch-Irish, German and Dutch came in droves. They chose to hack at the wilderness and bend it to their will. Cutting the great trees and killing the large predators and herbivores. Instead of living as part of the great circle they wanted to conquer it. It was one of the greatest culture clashes to ever take place in the history of the world. Yet it was the way of history. Conquer or be conquered.

This lifestyle also led to a religious clash also. Moneto versus God. Moneto had given this land to his red children to be shared with all and to live in harmony. God had given it to the whites to conquer and subdue. The whites in their superior thinking also saw their God as superior and tried to force their religion on the Native Americans. The other religious clash on the frontier was also Catholic against Protestantism. The French and Irish being good Catholics and the Protestants of Britain and other countries. This was evident when the early settlers of Marlinton, Marlin and Sewell migrated in and built a cabin and got along famously until They figure out one was a catholic and the other a Protestant. Sewell then moved into a sycamore across the stream from the Marlin cabin. They would check in each other each morning to make sure each was alive then would not speak again the rest of the day. Each got to meet their God however when they were wiped out during some late raids of the French Indian war.

These stories you are about to read are historical fiction. Some are adaptations of true stories and local legends. Some of them are purely fictional creation. The Rogers family you are being introduced to in this book is my family. I hope to write about them for many years as I have lived with their stories in my head and heart for a lifetime.

The places mentioned are real places. Every ridge, stream or rock ledge is somewhere I have visited. From the Kanawha Valley to the Ohio Valley at Pittsburgh, I have walked and studied these areas. I have hunted deer with the longrifle on the Buckhannon River. I have shot ducks and geese for Christmas dinners right in front of the site of Bush's Fort. I have dug ginseng in the Kanawha Valley and Campbell's Creek where Daniel Boone dug ginseng.

I have hunting land on the Middle Fork River. My family is from Braxton County on Cedar Creek not far from Strange Creek. I have trapped beavers on the mighty Elk River and its tributaries. I have walked these lands and lived these stories in my head since I was old enough to camp out in the rock ledge camps with my B.B. gun or homemade stick bows.

I hope in the coming years to fill in the family tree of the Rogers clan, telling stories as their family grows and migrates west. I hope you, the reader, enjoys the tales and possibly these stories will motivate you to study the history of the area you are in. To trace your ancestry. To get in touch with your roots and to realize where you came from and where you are going. To turn your thoughts inward and find your inner fire and to take better care of the earth you are given to live on. More importantly to live each day as if it were your last, life comes and goes like steam above a kettle.

Thanks for reading and welcome to my home, West Virginia, the Middle Ground.

Special thanks go out to Mike McWhorter, Roger Baker and others that have given of themselves to make this book a reality.

Table of Contents

Foreword

As you read "The Middle Ground," you will be transported back to a time of challenge and hardship. A time when the Appalachian Mountains were the new frontier. These early mountain men faced the unknown with courage and determination, some in search of a new life and some just fleeing an old life.

I am honored to write this foreword to Shon's first book of short stories. Shon has been intrigued with the history of the frontier since adolescence. I have often commented he may have been born about two hundred years too late. That however is not true, just as many things in life seem out of step in the present, we come to realize later that they were intended for just such a time as this. Shon is right on schedule to take you back in time with his research, realism, and added drama.

Find your easy chair and begin your very own exploration of the new frontier with these men of valor. Shon literally transports you into the unexplored wilderness of the untamed Appalachian Mountains, by presenting many of the accounts in the first-person narrative. When you are finished you may be ready to put on your buckskin, strap on your tomahawk, pick up your long rifle, and head out for your own mountain adventure.

John Butler
Father of the Author

" Morning
Smoke "

FJ Simms
5-16

Chapter 1
FRENCH AND OTTAWA ATTACK

The Ottawas were raiding up and down the western Virginia frontier with their French allies. The year 1754 has brought more war to this great new continent. France fighting England to control this massive country.

I am Chancy Rogers and I live on the great Elk River where the Holly River dumps in. It is a wild country full of bear and panthers. Indians prowl the mountains nearby.

I am friends of several of the Delaware tribe that hunt this ground. The Mingos come and go also. The Shawnee hunt here also and will lift your scalp if you are not careful. Me being an adopted brother to Chief Logan the Mingo doesn't mean a thing to those Shawnees.

I found this place by leaving Logan's encampment on the mouth of the Great Kanawha river. I followed the river up until I found this clear mountain river flowing out of the mountains, the Elk River. (Charleston, WV sits where the two great rivers meet.) I made my way another 50 to 60 miles up this beautiful river hunting and trapping as I went. The elk in this area are so fat and outstanding that one cow would provide enough meat for weeks. The elk growing fat from the tons of chestnuts dropped each fall in these mountains.

I caught beaver, otter and mink by the dozens. My pack horse was heavily laden with furs and plumes by the time I found the clear cold river called the Holly.

I carry a sail of canvass on my horse for a shelter. I carry two arms, a fine built .40 caliber rifle built by a Pennsylvania gun smith. I also carry a .62 caliber French Fusil for hunting and fighting purposes. It is good to roam these mountains with buck n ball in one hand and distance and accuracy in the other.

My possibles I carry in a canvass back pack. I carry buffalo hide bag with my balls and shot and other such small tools as needed. A horn of powder hangs from my other shoulder.

I wear an open front muslin shirt that hangs to my knees and tied with a bright blue woven belt. This shirt covers my deer skin breechclout and leggings. My pipe hawk is shoved down behind my belt in the back. My knife is sheathed and hangs around my neck. It is a simple knife of chestnut handle and long skinny blade perfect for fighting, skinning and scalping. On my feet are a pair of elk hide center seam moccasins. I have a tunic of Doe skin made by Logan's young sister that fancies me.

I have trapped this area and have come to know it well. Logan tells me that he will meet me at the confluence of these two streams on the new moon after the harvest moon. From here we will follow the mountains north to Old Town to trade my furs.

The appointed time came and I was sitting by the fire making some .40 caliber balls when Logan made his owl hoot from the dark. I hooted back and he came on in to the fire.

"You have comfortable camp here. We are not alone in this wilderness, 10 Ottawa and 3 Francois are raiding cabins from here to Kanawha. I have found one such cabin over on a creek that's banks are cedar lined and runs into the little Kanawha river."

"The Ottawa take 2 young girls for prisoner according to the signs."

Well now this got me to thinking. Two young ones in the hands of those devils. They were either going to become slaves of some Frenchy at Fort Duquesne or the Ottawa would enslave them or even eat them. They was known to do that every once in a while.

I think Logan knew what was in my mind, we immediately tore down my camp and started due west for the remains of the cabin. With luck the Ottawa and French would still be in the area planning to raid other cabins. We crossed several mountains as Logan led the way. The man was brilliant with direction in these mountains. A person could easily be distracted by the amazingly large chestnut, oak and Hemlock trees and get turned around to roam without direction.

As we slipped down the Cedar Creek after two days of traveling we came upon the cabin. A man and woman in their 20's had been killed and scalped. A baby less than one had her head bashed in. We picked up the trail and continued down the stream.

"They are following the stream. I know where we can cut miles off and be in front of them. We cross up and over here and drop onto a big trace then follow it down to the Cedar Creek and we may just be in front of them. There is a cabin at the mouth of where this big trace and a little trace come together. Maybe they know of it."

We did as Logan said. As we descended the ridge we got views of the cabin where two small streams met.

This family had a cornfield and garden. It was surrounded by sapling poles formed into a fence. A milk cow was visible. There was work going on in a field. Smoke was billowing into the sky where a man and boy were burning brush as they worked to clear another field in the turning leaves of autumn.

Logan and I split up. We knew each other well and he would give the call of a barred owl if he found anything, I was to do the same. He felt that we were there just in time.

As we started on our circuit that would bring us back together where we started Logan reminded me to slow down and look for ambush points as he had taught me.

2

I crept along and came to a crossing down-stream if the house. There in the mud with no attempt to be hidden were the tracks of four Ottawas and two Frenchmen. I backed off and hooted. Logan showed up several minutes later. I showed him the tracks.

Logan read the sign then said, " they will creep into the cornfield and wait until the man is coming from the new field to attack. "

I told Logan that I had found a rock cliff with a clear view of the corn field. I could crawl up there and watch for the first sign of attack and try to pick one or two off. Logan could go to the other side of the cabin and lay in wait until my first shot was fired. When the attackers came out he would engage them from there. I would run down and join the fray from behind, hoping our distraction gave the settler time to understand the peril.

I snaked my way to rock cliff and I crawled to the edge keeping out of sight. I peered down and it took me a few minutes to spot a Frenchman down behind a fence post and an Ottawa laying beside of him.

The distance was 75 yards. That's not a far piece for my rifle especially shooting at a man. I pulled the hammer back and set the rear trigger. I said a little prayer as I squeezed easily on the front trigger. The flint struck the frizzen making a shower of sparks. The hesitation from that until the charge went off seemed longer than the split second that it took. The ball traveled and took the Frenchman at the base of the skull, killing him instantly. I left my rifle and ran with my Fusil and tomahawk into the fray. War cries were being screamed out as the Ottawas attacked. I hit the corn patch on full bore and saw an Indian rise in front of me. I pointed the Fusil and pulled the trigger. The load of buck and ball pretty much tore him in half.

I dropped the Fusil and pulled my hawk and my knife. A Frenchman stood in my path. He was aiming a musket at me. Just as he pulled the trigger I dropped and rolled at him. The shot missed high by a foot or more. As I can to my feet my momentum took me past him, I slammed the tomahawk into his spine then with a flick of the knife I slit his throat from ear to ear.

I heard Logan's musket go off and knew that two enemies remained. As I rounded the cabin Logan was engaged with a portly Ottawa and the other brave was trying to slam his tomahawk into the boy's head. The homesteader was down already with blood on his forehead. The brave heard me coming and let the boy lose. He came at me and made a full round house swing with his hawk. I ducked it and countered it with a swing of my own making a glancing blow off his shoulder. We came together then knife to knife.

I slowly but surely started to win the strength contest. My knife went between his ribs into his heart as he stared wickedly into my eyes. As he faltered with my knife in his chest, I took a step back and slammed the tomahawk into his temple.

3

I turned in time to see Logan dispatching the huge Ottawa with his war club.

Luckily the homesteader was just stunned. In the span of one and half minutes we had killed 4 braves and two Frenchies. We quickly explained to the homesteader and his wife what was happening. We knew we had to immediately go after the other six Ottawas. The sound of the skirmish would send them on their way with the two captive girls.

I recovered the Fusil and my rifle and reloaded. We took our scalps and hit the trail on the run. The settler agreed to keep my horse and pelts as now we were running on the trail.

As we ran down the Cedar Creek catching partial tracks now here and there as they tried to cover their trail. Logan came up with another plan.

"Let us circle them again, I know a trail where we can get around them and be waiting at the mouth of this cedar creek and ambush them there. It is better to choose the place of battle."

My fear was they may kill the two girls and travel faster. Logan thought that they wouldn't do that until they reached the little Kanawha river and any surviving members of their party showed.

We circled. Logan set the pace and that man could run. We knew we had to cover twenty miles in short but steep, rattlesnake and copperhead infested mountains. Our plan was to not take a break until we arrived at the mouth of the Cedar Creek.

We arrived and found two dug-out canoes hidden. We knew their plan well. We looked the area over and found that cedar creek flowed between two mountains that provided a great ambush point. We settled in about fifty yards from each other creating a crossfire on the Indian trail.

It took a full day before an Ottawa scout showed. He was very careful. We let him pass and check on the dug outs. As he went back up the trail to the others, we checked our charges and our weapons.

Logan carried a British trade musket and a war club with a round piece of granite in a dried rawhide pouch on the end. He could quickly dispatch any human with that club.

He had a deep burgundy print shirt. A red wool breechclout and fine elk-skin leggings. His knife was a trade knife with a red painted handle. His hawk was also a pipe hawk but was so much more ornamental than mine. He had gotten it as a teenager fighting Cherokees in the south.

He had a deep blue wool blanket about him for warmth.

We didn't have to wait long. The scout came back leading the other five and the two girls.

We let the scout pass as well as the brave leading the two girls. I picked out the brave furthest back and shot him through the chest with my rifle. The others froze for a split second allowing us to get shots off with our muskets.

4

We rushed in and I saw Logan obliterate a braves head with his war club. I went hand to hand with a brave carrying a rifle stock war club. He hit me a glancing blow on my left shoulder making my hand go numb and I dropped my knife. The brave was in close to me trying to hit me with his club, my right hand loosed from his and I swung my hawk hard and drive it 4 inches deep into his temple.

As I rolled up I saw Logan jump another brave from behind and pretty much decapitate him with a slice of his trade knife.

The scout and the injured warrior who was leading the girls had dropped their rope and got to the dugout making their escape.

Logan and I got our breath and untied the girls. Dennison was their name one 12 and one 14. We decided to take them back to the settler Bogg's cabin on the big trace and recover my horse.

As we headed to Wheeling by way of the Little Kanawha and the Ohio. We stood on a bluff over-looking that great river. Logan looked at me and wondered, " What is to become of me and my white brother. This frontier is a bloody ground, meant only for hunting and trapping. It hurts Logan to kill his red brothers that are only trying to protect what has always been used by us. I have given my word to always be friends of the whites but I have a vision of dark days. Many whites will die and Logan holds a bloody tomahawk."

I told him that maybe his vision is not accurate and I hoped in the future my Red brother and I would never fight each other. We continued on to Old Town.

"Startling
Quiet"
5/15 RJ Simons

Chapter 2
THE FRENCHMAN'S TREASURE

My name is Simon de Jesame. I grew up near the city of Montreal and was recruited to be part of a 250 man flotilla that will head to the meeting of the waters of the Allegheny and Monongehela rivers where the great Ohio starts. We are to lay claim by burying lead plates along the way with tree markers at main water intersections. We are to take the great Ohio to the Miamisepe river, then up to the Great Lakes and back to Montreal.

Our crew is led by Baron Celeron de Brienville. I have been hired to hunt and scout. I grew up doing such in the woods surrounding Montreal. Who knows, I may see land worth settling into and be rid of this crew.

As we set off from Montreal I notice that a Captain of the army is in charge of two very heavy trunks. One I know contains the leaden plates. The other I find out has one plate of gold and three of silver! If a man could escape into the wilderness with these he would be a wealthy man. Ahhh to disappear into the wilderness and return in a couple years under a different name and with newly minted gold and silver bars! One would have all the women and drink he wanted!

I am well outfitted for this trip. I wear a very nice set of deep blue wool leggings that come to my mid-thigh. I wear a matching breechclout. I have a belt of intricate quilling made by a Mohawk woman, she also quilled a matching set of leg ties. I wear a long shirt made of a calico print. Over this when it's cold I wear a blanket coat of the same deep blue wool as my leggings. My moccasins are heavy moose and are sewed up the center with a seam. I carry a canvass bag with all my possibles and I carry a wool blanket and bit of canvass around my shoulder for my bed.

I am well armed. My Fusil de Chasse is a .69 calibre and the wood has a brilliant blue paint coat on it. I also carry a knife in my leather belt and a long handle simple tomahawk. I wear a blue wool voyagers hat. With what I wear and carry I am confident to survive the wilds of western Virginia or the Ohio lands.

As we near the meeting place of rivers in this summer of 1749. I have made great acquaintance with the Captain who cares for the previous plates. I have given extra of my kills to him and at times I have given him small fur trinkets of animals I have killed along this trip. I have even volunteered to watch the plates at night when he slipped off to the Delaware villages to see the maidens. Soon I will make my getaway. Soon Simon de

Jesame will be a rich man.

As we floated idly on the mighty Ohio we have buried one leaden plate. Celeron has threatened a group of English traders. I am concerned because the silver and gold plates are to be buried in special places, chosen by Celeron. Soon he will start to choose these. I will make my get away at the mouth of the river the Shawnees call the Little Kanawha. From a Delaware I learned to follow this river to its head and I would be in a place that I could hunt and live.

As we arrived at the Little Kanawha I learn the Celeron will bury a silver plate here! I must make my move tonight and be away! Luckily Celeron breaks out the good wine the night before the plate ceremony!

As the evening festivity begins I give my share to the good Captain. Soon he is drunk and the key to the trunk is mine. I have located a good carry basket with a forehead strap. Quickly I open the trunk and move the plates into the basket. It weighs a good one hundred plus pounds. I slip away into the darkness and begin up the river.

My plan is to travel the first forty-eight hours solid, making time on the party. Celeron is no idiot he will have a crew after me to recover this treasure. I need distance as it is my friend. Keeping the river on my right and pacing myself, the miles begin to pass quickly. Growing up in the bush around Montreal, I have lived off the land my whole life. I will need to make a hastily put together bow and some arrows so that I may hunt quietly. The shot from my Fusil will attract any followers to my location.

As darkness turns to daylight, I have forded Mill Run and two other streams. Exhaustion is setting in. I know soon I will have to take a break and hunt for food. As I come up to Walker Creek at the noon high sun, I find a bark canoe! What luck.

I quickly load my pack and musket into the canoe and push off into the current. With a canoe I will be able to put distance from myself and pursuit. Then stomach falls, what if Celeron orders a party up the river in a canoe or bateaux? They will be on me soon or possible even now ahead of me setting up an ambush!

I immediately cross the river and paddle up the western bank. If they think me afoot, they will assume I am on the eastern side. I set a rhythm with the paddle and put another fifteen miles behind me by nightfall.

I do not risk a fire this night. It is June but a cool fog sets into the Little Kanawha valley. I spend an uncomfortable night in the cool with mosquitoes eating me alive.

I start out well before dawn. This day I must find food and I must build a bow. I whittle myself a set of straight fishing hooks out of a hard wood with thorns. I found some grubs and I fish along the way. I catch a drum and a catfish nearly as long as my leg, this evening I will eat good.

I cover many more miles this day and I come to a huge bend in the river. The ridge above me on my left has to look down on river I have already covered. I can hide my canoe and hike to the ridge and watch my back trail. I can build a fire and eat.

I eat my fill of catfish and dry what is remaining over the fire. I sleep well. As the sun rises I am eating more and packing to go back to the canoe. As it becomes bright I see on the river two canoes filled Indians! They are coming in hard and I assume they are coming after me!

I gathered my things and run to the canoe, I will have a good hour lead on them but they have the advantage of having several paddlers. Unbeknownst to me this group of Shawnees had come across the five men who were trailing me and killed and scalped them all. The canoe I am in was one of theirs and they are not happy.

The miles fly by. I do not stop. I paddle day and night, eating the fish I have left. I paddle for three days straight and part of a fourth. I am tired and hungry. I finally encounter a water falls (Falls Mill in modern Braxton County, WV) and decide from here I will follow the stream by land. I gather my pack and my musket and head out.

After a haggard run of over seventy-five miles I finally reach where this stream is small and clear. I can step across it in many places. I continue on and collapse at a rock face with a small over hang. No fire during this rest. I can feel my enemies closing. I must hide this treasure!

I sleep sound, the sleep of an overly exhausted man who has dropped his guard. A rustle in the night and a sharp pain in my thigh! I awake to an arrow protruding from my left thigh. I swing my Fusil and fire. I hear a scream and another Shawnee fires his rifle at me. I rolled out of the way just in time. I grab my belongings and stumble into the night.

Quickly I reload with ball and buck. I quickly pull the arrow, luckily it wasn't deep. The wound scares me for infection. I limp along and circle around to watch my back trail. The Shawnees are right on me!

I take off up the mountain, leaking blood and getting weaker. I leave my little stream and cross a ridge and drop into a beautiful river that is clear and cold (the Buckhannon River near Alexander). I follow this stream down while hiding my trail. My followers cannot be far behind. I find a mountain brook that puts into this river and I start to hike up it. Maybe this will throw the Shawnees off my trail for a while.

I need to hide this treasure and find food. I have not ate in a week. I have to recover. My leg is sore and stiff. As I get towards the top of this next mountain there is a large rock overhang darkened with the soot of many fires. (present day Indian Camp, Upshur County, WV) I scramble around and find a rock pile in the forest. I rearrange the rocks and hide the treasure here. I carve a cross in the tree not ten paces away. Now I can move more freely.

I continue on out the ridge for three miles feeling the noose tightening. I can start to see glimpses of the Shawnee behind me. I come out into a small meadow that has a rocky center. I can hear the river below. (Big Bend near present day Sago) I rush into the rocks as I hear a rifle shot. I lay in the rocks with my Fusil. I fire as one Shawnee shows himself.

As I am reloading they rush from all directions at once. I pull my knife and tomahawk and wade into them. I plunge my knife into a brawny chest. I hit a forehead with my tomahawk. I am grabbed by strong hands and taken to the ground. I feel knives plunging into my body! I feel a knife across my forehead as a Shawnee screams with my scalp in his hand. I feel a burning in my belly and see a Shawnee holding my entrails as he yells in my face. I am starting to fade as the biggest Shawnee slams his war club into my temple putting me out of my misery.

I, Simon de Jesame, have stolen and hidden a treasure to be found by someone luckier than me. Will it be you?

Chapter 3
THE PRINGLE BROTHERS -
FIRST WHITE SETTLERS OF THE BUCKHANNON

My name is Samuel Pringle, the year is 1761 and my brother John and I are garrisoned here at Fort Pitt.

What a muddy hell this is. We work all day with little rations. Everyone here has the flux, the Indians are all diseased and try anything to barter for everything you own. The commander of this Fort always has drilling and marching. We are not British regulars but we are expected to act, march and discharge our duties as such.

I was at the river front the other day when by chance I met Chancy Rogers just coming in to trade furs. He told me of the mountains to the south and clean rivers.

He told me of timber a man cannot reach around, bears and buffalo along the rivers, deer and elk in the mountains. He told me the Middle Ground was a heaven on earth if you could friend and live as the Indians.

I went to my brother John who was suffering from flux awful bad. I passed on all this and told him we should desert and be away from this diseased Fort. He was leery as to deserting. If caught we would be hung immediately with no court martial. I told him we needed to plan well and be gone.

For the next month we hoarded rations. We packed our issue haversacks with food, string and extra clothing. We rolled away a couple extra wool blankets. I traded a stolen British officers gorget to a Delaware for a French Fusil de Chasse of .62 caliber and hid it away.

John and I swiped some powder horns from the commissary and hid those. John came up with a cut off British musket of .69 caliber. My final step was to trade John's scarlet militia coat for a canoe that would carry us both and our cache up the Monongahela river.

The cold night came when we must leave. The food situation at the Fort had worsened. John's flux was starting to drain the life from him. At the guard change that night we snuck out. We immediately went to where our canoe was hidden. John and I quickly loaded all our goods and pushed off.

At first the going was tough. The Monongahela was flowing swift and muddy. The early February flow coming out of the mountains was great. Once we figured the canoe out we started making time. We had decided we would paddle all night and into the afternoon before setting a camp for food and rest. We needed distance from the Fort.

12

It was cold that night and John was bundled in a wool blanket since we had traded his uniform. I had on my scarlet wool coat but our faces and ears became numb without protection from the wind.

We knew nothing of this wilderness.

After three days on the river we did venture to shoot some ducks. We had chosen our weapons for their availability also because we could load them with buck or ball and at times with both. John being in front took down a brace of ducks and a large white swan that day. That night we fed well upon them as we built a warm fire.

So went the days on this river. Never once seeing a living person either white or red. We killed deer several times and smoked the venison against harder times. We also worked the green hides each time we stopped.

We grew up on the South Branch of the Potomac river. We knew fishing, hunting and trapping. We would have to hunt and trap enough hides and furs to make new clothes as these military issue were not sufficient for the wilderness.

The miles went and when we arrived at a place where another great river entered the Monongahela we decided to take it. That did not last long as this river, that we guessed to be the Cheat, was to rugged with swift water to take the canoe upstream. We loaded our few belongings on our back and continued on. Our goal was a river that came into the Cheat that would lead us deep into the Middle Ground. After 7 days of walking and wandering a little we came to the river we were looking for. (Tygart River)

We went up this new river several miles and made camp. We had found a beaver pond nearby and I fashioned three deadfalls with fresh cut black birch as the bait stick.

John's flux had cleared on this new diet of wild meat and pure water. He was feeling more like his old self. By the time I got back from setting deadfalls, John had a fire going, a tent set up made from the half sail we scrounged up. He had a turkey going on the spit.

"Brother, we need new clothes and we need shelter. This winter is far from over, the cold will set in again." He was right. We made a plan to stay here a couple of days and try for some beaver. Also we would hunt for a couple days here for a couple bear. We needed some fat meat to get heat in our bodies. We also needed the bear skins to make some coats. One of the best things I had swiped at the Fort was needles, awl and several rolls of course thread. We would also keep the tendons and silverskin covering from our bears and deer to make a strong string and thread. I had made sure to bring a large kettle and several small iron hooks for catching turtles and fish.

John had been set against extra weight but I convinced him otherwise about the need for a few extras. It could be we have to live our life out in these mountains.

The next day I checked the deadfalls and I caught one small beaver. I reset and headed up a mountain close by. There I found a good pile of chestnuts to make a warm soup out of. I headed back to the camp.

John had killed a bear some distance away and had brought the heavy hide and all the best cuts of meat. We kept the claws and teeth of the bears as trade items also as button material if need be. We stretched the bear hide and fleshed it good with our knives. We had no salt but would try to get a decent tan with the bears brain without the salt. I had heard from a Seneca when I was younger about tanning with the bark of an oak. We would have to try this. That night we feasted on bear, the choice cuts of the beaver and the skinned and roasted beavertail. I had also made a thick porridge out of the chestnuts.

That night it snowed. The wind shifted from a southwest to a north by west and the snow from this storm hit with a rush. The next day would be a camp day for sure.

After 2 weeks in the Tygart camp we went on. Each clothed in a new bearskin coat and leggings. We each had a beaver pelt hood and mitts. We continued in the snow. Further up the Tygart River we went until we came upon another nice river flowing in. This was in a remote canyon and we made our camp overlooking this junction. We made another camp here on a rock ledge overlooking the canyon. Using our half sail and the ledge we had a palace in these mountains.

John had started hunting more and more as he had completely regained his strength. I was feeling stronger than I had in years. There was a pureness to this air and no disease whatsoever.

I found several shoots of elderberry. I took these stalks to camp and began to fashion short hollowed out tubes. When I had about 20 done I took up a deerskin pack full of something very valuable we had been keeping.

Out of every deer and bear we had killed, I had extracted the bladder and emptied it, turning it inside out I blew it full of air and tied it off. These had dried. Now I had a dozen small containers for liquid. I took my elderberry tubes and went to a sugar maple grove and I carefully drilled into the tree with my knife until I could insert the tube and hang a bladder on the tube. John and I would have sugar now.

Where goes the time? We spent a full year in this area, the next year we spent roaming the length of another river that we discovered. (Middle Fork). 1764 was approaching, it had been 3 years since our desertion. We decided we had to have a more permanent home as our sailcloth had given way during the last great snow. In three years of hunting and trapping this area we had run into no Indians, we hated to leave it but we were having to hunt harder for game and food also.

We headed up the river whose mouth we had lived on for two years and more. (Buckhannon River). This river valley leveled out more so than the Tygart and the Middle Fork. We had to keep our eyes out for

14

a cave or something similar to set up permanent residence in, seeing how we only had tomahawks we could not build a cabin.

I had long studied the Delaware huts around Fort Pitt. They would pull de real saplings over and lash them together making a frame. Then they would cover this with overlapping bark creating a waterproof hut. We pushed on up this new land.

The game was unbelievable. Deer and bears were seen frequently. Elk roamed the higher peaks and ridges and buffalo sign was everywhere. The river was full of fish and abundant waterfowl.

We pushed on camping and hunting. We had accumulated quite the bale of furs and hides. We had made a sled to pull our belongings on and this was tiring.

We were finding no shelter or caves near water! This was disappointing. John and I would have to build that Delaware style hut soon and settle in. We came upon a creek entering the Buckhannon river from the west. We decided to rest here for a day or two. John went up the creek to hunt and I crossed the creek to continue up the river for a scout.

I had turned into a true savage. I had not a stitch of civilized clothes on. I had on buckskin moccasins and leggings. I wore a buckskin breechclout, over this I had a knee length tunic of doeskin. I had a bearskin coat and on my head was a beaver pelt hood. The last three years had really changed our ward robe.

I started up the steep bank of the creek where it entered the river and there before me was a mighty sycamore standing well over a hundred feet tall. This tree was immense and had three trunks coming up from an immense swelling at the level of the ground. I walked around the base and on the river side an opening in the base! I quickly struck a fire with flint and steel and made a torch. I reached in cautiously to make sure a sleeping bear was not inside. I crawled in and stood up in an amazing eight feet by eight feet room! Completely weather tight. I held the torch high and the ceiling was some nine feet high. I had found our new home.

John soon returned with a couple turkeys. He was amazed and moved with emotion that God had given us a home. We quickly moved in. The first thing we did was to take stones and clay from the riverbank and we built a fireplace with a chimney. After two days of hard work we finally figure on how to make it draw.

John made two low cots out of our sled while I made a chair that could be used to reach the high reaches of our interior. I wedged saplings up near the ceilings to hang meat on that had been cured. We moved our pelts and hides in and made warm comfortable beds.

What a country we had roamed into. The creek our tree was on we named Turkey Run. You could go up it and kill a turkey or two within minutes. The next creek that flowed into the Buckhannon upstream was full of beaver. We had found a buffalo jawbone in the mud at the mouth of the stream and thus we named this stream, Jawbone.

15

We made pounds of maple sugar in our kettle. Then on one of our several week-long treks we located a spring on another river miles away that contained salt. We returned there with our kettle and boiled down several pounds of salt. (Webster Springs on the Elk River).

We lived good but for two fears. Indians and our powder and lead running low. After two good years in our tree, we had tomahawked claimed acres and acres of land and had made our plans on living here permanent. We knew that at least one of us would have to make a run for powder and lead. It was decided that John would take a large bale of furs and travel due east until he hit the southern branch of the Potomac river. Here he would travel until encountering a town or post to trade the furs for what we needed and return across land as quick as possible. John also took my deerskin with a map of the Middle Ground we had been exploring going on five years now. He would add to it or use it if necessary.

The next morning John took off and I was alone. I spent the next week exploring a canyon not far away that was full of ginseng and ramps. This was a steep country. (Stonecoal Creek) The stream was clear and full of many colorful trout. I would gorge myself in the evening with fish and ramps. I found the big yellow morel mushrooms that we came to like growing here. They covered these hill sides. It was a good time but I had only enough powder for five more shots and only 3 round balls and a small amount of buck shot left. If John did not return soon I would be surviving with longbow and club.

As I was coming down one of those steep hillsides my moccasined foot slipped and I felt my leg snap between a log and a rock. I rolled to the bottom. My head was spinning with pain. My leg was broke and I was at least five miles as a crow flies from the tree probably a good eight to nine miles away.

I got as comfortable as I could and looked over my situation. I found a couple sapling I could reach and with my tomahawk I fashioned a couple splints. Every pound with that hawk jarring my shattered leg with pain.

I crawled over to the stream edge and wedged my leg between two rocks, I pulled gently in severe pain, passing out twice until my leg was set as good as I could get it. I splinted it and wrapped the splinting with rawhide.

My best bet was to get back to our tree. There I had food and constant water. I could also fish for food. I decided to start crawling. After the first one hundred yards I was torn up from the rocks and cold from the damp soil. I had to keep going.

I crawled what seemed a mile but was only five hundred yards and passed out. I don't know how long I had been this way but I was awakened by a cold nose and a warm tounge! There was a bear smelling and licking me. When I opened my eyes he stepped back. I grabbed my Fusil and held it on him and talked to him about the need for him to go.

He backed off and sat on his haunches licking his great paw. I started crawling again. I topped onto a flat plain and crawled. I hit a swampy stream and knew that this creek flowed into the Jawbone creek about three miles away. I kept on.

Now funny thing was that old bear kept following me to. At the end of the third day I began to feel a fever taking me. I chilled and began coughing, my lungs full of fluid. I was coming down with pleurisy. I passed out in a shivering fit on the cold April soil.

I awoke with a start. That old bear was curled up next to me keeping me warm! I started crawling again. Later that day I tried eating a couple dried ramps from my possible bag and some jerky. I found a small amount of maple sugar and gave it to the bear.

That night passed out and cold again, the bear got close and slept against me. I did not know if I was in delirium or not but in the middle of the night I heard the bear growling at two wolves that were getting close to me.

The next morning I crawled on. After several days of the cold and crawling, I finally arrived back to the tree. I threw my new friend a good amount of our sugar as I kindled a fire. I passed out again from the fever and liquid filled lungs. I was close to death.

I made a tea from ginseng, mullein and maple sugar and sipped this. The whole time giving my new friend some dried fish and sugar. The days passed into a couple months. The old bear stayed with me providing me someone to talk to while I healed. After six weeks I got myself a crutch built and wandered around. After twelve weeks I could take a few steps.

After four months my leg was healed somewhat but I was out of powder and lead. I had used my last rounds on ducks, geese and a few pigeons. My food supply was running low. The pneumonia had taken pounds from me and my energy. I would talk to the old bear telling him how lucky he was that I did not have a round left for him and was too weak to pull a bow. If John did not get back soon he would not find much of me left.

I was laying outside in the warm sun of an autumn day. I was sinking in and out of delirium. I had not long on this earth.

My bear who came to me many months ago was sleeping nearby. He suddenly came awake and stood on his hind feet and looked around sniffing the wind. He suddenly bolted away! It was then I heard a familiar voice yelling, " Hello the camp!" Then in strode John with a big pack on his shoulders. I began to cry.

Good old John had returned. He nursed me back to health over the next few weeks. He had told me that he looked for my bear and found no tracks anywhere near-by. That the old bear was a figment of my imagination and delirium.

The other news that John brought was that we were no longer fugitives. The war was over and we could return to our childhood home. I contemplated that and agreed but we both knew we would be back to this Eden and when we returned we would bring back friends and family and settle this country.

We began the trek to the Potomac valley in the spring. As we topped a ridge, I turned back and looked at our tree and the valley of the Buckhannon and knew I would return and my bones would lay here permanently someday.......

Chapter 4
JEREMIAH "CAT" ROGERS EARNS HIS NAME

I had went to sleep after a hard day of grubbing stumps and had slept the sleep of the dead. My Father, John Rogers, was a stickler for hard work, I did not mind it so much as it was making me stronger.

He would work me until an hour before supper time and then release me to the forest. I always had that hour to myself to run and explore around our Virginia home here on the Eastern side of the Blue Ridge.

I am Jeremiah Rogers and I am fourteen years old. I had been grubbing stumps and shooting game with my .40 caliber rifle since I was ten and we moved down into this country from the Chesapeake Bay Area.

I woke with a start as I heard voices down below in our cabin. I peeked over the edge of the loft and there he was, my Uncle Chancy. Chancy was the youngest of my Pa's brothers. He had left home about the same age as I am now. He had went to sea on schooner running molasses from the Caribbean to Philadelphia. He then had saved enough money for himself to buy a good rifle and outfit himself with trade goods and head into the West and start trapping and trading with the Indians.

He had lived for the last fifteen years from Fort Pitt all the way down to the cane fields of Kentucky. Sometimes it was a couple years before we would hear from him, there was a time or two my Pa had even wondered out loud if Chancy had been killed by red boogers but that was not the case and he always seemed to show up.

He had made friends with the Delaware Chief Buckhongehalas and also the Mingo Chief Logan. He had lived in peace with them and enjoyed his time in what he called the "Middle Ground". When he needed money or goods he would ride into a post and trade furs, hides and pelts. He lived a care free life and I envied him.

I flipped down out of that loft and was all smiles. He slammed me on the back a time or two and looked me up and down. "Boy, you look to be twenty years old!" He was right. This farming and grubbing stumps ages you up pretty quick.

Chancy was there to talk to my father about my future. He wanted to take me on a hunting trip on the far side of the mountains. Maybe even find some land to claim. His idea was to take two riding horses and a pack animal and cross the Blue Ridge and a couple other ranges and hit the Greenbrier River valley. Then ride north and cross a divide and drop into the Tygart River valley, here he wanted to hunt and trap all the way to the

Cheat then head to Fort Pitt to sell and trade out and make a ride for home. Letting myself see and study the country.

My Ma did not like it none to much but what was a boy of fourteen to do in 1770? Just sit at home and be a dirt farmer and let all the good land be claimed? My Pa relented after some smooth talking by Chancy and myself. Pa just figured I would run off anyways and he was probably right. The one day a week hunting and the one hour per evening on the other nights was getting boring. I wanted to go out and prove myself.

Chancy had a beautiful grey riding mare but he was most proud of his little pack mule. He said that animal had never quit him and was nigh as old as I was. Pa let me have the chestnut riding mare. We packed up what we would need and planned on heading out the next morning.

It was a warm morning with the humid feel of thunderstorms in the air, it was towards the end of the month of August. Chancy was wanting to be in a good hunting area by middle of September to the first part of October.

I had packed my belongings quickly the night before. I had changed out of my homespun pants for my deerskin leggings and breechclout that I always wore hunting. Then I wore a long muslin hunters shirt that tied about me. I wore simple center seam moccasins. My hat was black beaver felt and very wide brimmed. The side above my right eye was pinned up with a writing quill and a wing-bone Turkey call. I carried behind my saddle a wool blanket with a wool hunting frock wrapped in it. Chancy said we would make our own heavier winter clothing as we killed and trapped the animals necessary.

I had my fine .40 caliber Pennsylvania rifle, I also carried a plain tomahawk that my Pa had pounded out at the forge. My knife was simple and forged also. About nine inches of blade with hickory scale handles. It was in a rawhide sheath and tucked in behind my belt. I carried my calf skin possible bag that I had made after a bear had killed the milk cow's calf two years ago. I also had a canvass haversack hanging over my shoulder. I threw one small iron pot and my copper mug down into a set of canvass bags that was filled with camp supplies and hung behind my saddle.

With my goodbyes we were off. What a grand adventure for a fourteen year old! We passed several cabins and a couple settlements. We crossed the Blue Ridge and looked out across a great expanse of mountains and land. We camped by streams filled with incredible fish and turtles. Then we climbed another mountain and stopped on its crest looking over the country. Chancy informed me we was a sitting on the Allegheny Front. All the water behind us went to the Atlantic, while all the water in front of us went to the Ohio then on down to the Gulf of Mexico. Also, once we went started down the mountain we would be breaking crown law because we were heading in the Middle Ground that was the buffer between red man and white, agreed upon in a treaty signed in 1763. Off we rode.

21

We unsheathed our rifles from the long cases they were in. Now our focus on watching for Indians was even greater. We were always checking to our priming and making sure knife and tomahawk were at hand.

After the second camp and dropping into the Middle Ground we finally rode into the valley of the Greenbrier River. The river was low and easy to cross. This was a dry time of year in these mountains. We hit upon a trail after crossing the river. Chancy said that this was the Warriors Trail that ran from Canada to the Carolinas and even further south. (U.S. 219 follows this trail through West Virginia) we followed the trail north. Chancy explained that mostly the Senecas use this trail and they had calmed down a bit towards us whites since the French-Indian war. Settlements were still sparse in this area after the Marlin family had pulled out or was murdered.

We rode up and camped on another divide between the Greenbrier River and the Tygart.

It was a grand life. Hunting, trapping and fishing the streams. Putting up pelts and hides that I would be able to trade later. The stars at night were amazing and seemed like they were just above these mountain tops at night.

The next morning we dropped in the Tygart Valley. We rode a good twenty miles and decided to make a base camp where a mountain stream came down and joined the river. (Mill Creek). Chancy took some time and mapped out the rivers and how they laid. I was always busy transferring these maps onto a deerskin map of the whole country I had been working on. We decided that we would each go a different way and explore and hunt for the next month. Tomorrow would be the Harvest moon and each of us would return here on the next full moon.

The plan was that Chancy would take the horses and mule down the Tygart and cross some mountains and work his way to the head of the Cheat River. He wanted to run a line of marten, fisher and ermine traps, as these were bringing the best trades. He was hoping at the high elevations the ermine would be turning their winter white.

I would take this creek up the mountain and cross into the upper Buckhannon River drainage and hunt and trap for beaver on mountain streams putting into the Buckhannon. Then circle around to the head of the Middle Fork and back into Tygart's Valley.

The next morning I took off on foot as Chancy took off with the animals. I ascended the mountain along the creek. That night I camped out under the stars with wolves sounding off in all directions.

As I started walking the next morning I heard a bull elk bugle in front of me. I made a stalk and came on an edge of a meadow. There was a nice bull and several cows. I picked out a spring calf and pulled the trigger. The calf fell in a heap, my round ball breaking it's neck. I took the choice cuts and wrapped them in the hide and continued on. I hit the Buckhannon that evening and made Camp. I staked out the Elk skin and started scraping it. I cooked up a good dinner of elk tongue, heart and inner loins.

I started down the Buckhannon the next morning. I passed several small streams that looked promising, however the beaver sign just was not great. I covered a good eight miles that day before making camp for the night. I roasted an elk back strap and ate two brook trout I had caught out of the river. The next morning I was up and walking again. Paying attention closely for cuttings on trees and looking for beaver dams.

As the Buckhannon River widened, I came upon the mouth of a stream that had several chewed sticks. Definitely beaver in this small stream. I laid out my deerskin and pondered on it. This stream looked to be Laurel Run. It was one of the streams that Chancy had me draw on the map. It was only about four to five miles long but at its Head you crossed a low gap and you could drop to the Middle Fork River on the other side of the mountain.

I started up the stream. I had made it about two miles when I came upon the first beaver dam. I got into my haversack and proceeded to make snares with the rawhide cord I always carried with me. It took me the better part of the day to set the snares. Then as twilight started to settle in I took the three highly valuable forged steel foothold traps out of my haversack and set them with newly birch sticks as bait.

I followed a small stream in a hollow up a couple flats of the mountain and found a rock ledge to make camp under. I built up a good reflector with all the loose flat rock laying around and settled in for the night.

The next morning found me improving my shelter. I walled it in completely with rock and downed logs. I pretty much had a one room cabin built. After putting a couple hours in with my shelter, I walked to check the snares and traps. I had caught a beaver in a snare and one in a foothold.

I pulled one foothold and put it in my haversack. I then retreated back to my shelter and skinned the two beavers out. I carefully fleshed them with a flint scraper I had knapped at home a couple years before. I then made a couple hoops out of black alder and I carefully hooped those two beavers up to dry.

I carefully removed all the meat off each beaver and I made a dish out of clay and put the beaver meat inside and closed off the clay dish completely enveloping the beaver. I then dug a hole in my fire pit and buried the clay and covered it with hot coals. I would dig it up that evening and break the clay open and have a hot steaming meal of clay baked beaver.

I then carefully removed the castor glands from the beavers and taking mud that I had carried up from the beaver pond I grounded and pounded the concoction together until I had a smelly mess of castor mud. I had hollowed out an elderberry bush section about ten inches long. I crammed as much of the smelly concoction as I could into the make shift container. I then grabbed my rifle and set out further up the Laurel Run.

I came upon another beaver pond about a mile above the other. Here I set snares and I made a castor mound set with the one foothold trap. I then made three deadfalls with large flat rocks using the castor as bait.

After setting the snares I cut up through some of the largest sugar maple I had ever seen and found myself in a sea of yellow and red. Ginseng! These were all huge four and five prong plants. My Uncle Chancy had told me to keep my eyes open and to dig as much as I could stand to carry. I got down there and commenced to digging.

After about two hours my stomach was calling to me to head back to the shelter. I had dug about thirty roots that were amazing specimens.

I arrived back to the shelter and dug up the clay pot and cracked it open. The small shelter filled with the amazing smell of baked beaver stewing in its own grease. A meal fit for a king.

The next morning I collected another five beavers from the two ponds. I dug more ginseng and right before dark that night I killed a nice size bear. I skinned him out and took all his best cuts and hide back to the shelter. I could see a good warm bear skin in my future.

After a week I had accumulated eleven beaver pelts, one bear, two whitetail deerskins and a wolf that I caught in a deadfall that I had baited with beaver carcasses. I had made a fair amount of jerky and had a good string of ginseng root hanging and drying in my shelter. The next day I was going to push all the way to the head of Laurel Run and do some exploring.

I packed my deerskin in my haversack to add to the map as I went. I put a little jerky in there as well. I grabbed my rifle, checked to the priming and took off.

After a couple hours of steady climbing I topped out on a beautiful chestnut covered ridge. I started following the ridge to the east and after about a mile I decided to pick up some chestnut and make a deer jerky and chestnut gruel for my dinner. I leaned my rifle up against a tree and was down on my knees. Every few minutes I would still scan the woods for trouble. I had seen no sign of Indians on this trip and even though Chancy said this was Delaware territory and they were friendly, I did not want to be surprised.

I was just about done with my chestnut gather when I caught a flash out of the corner of my eye. Something jumped on my back and I felt claws tear into my back and teeth rip at me neck! I tried to throw the animal off and made it on one knee and drew my knife. It was a panther. I rolled, fighting the cat as he bit and scratched me over and over. Temporarily we separated and he hit me again. I felt my knee wrench and buckle. I stabbed him hard with my knife. His mouth closed down on my arm as I was holding him away from my neck. I stabbed that cat I don't know how many times. I tried to roll away and the cat snarled and bit down on the back of my skull, shredding a piece of scalp with the bite. I got up on one knee, blood pouring into my eyes. The cat was circling but was injured bad also. He tried to rush me one more time and I met him with all the strength I had left, jamming my knife home through his sternum into his heart, I held him tight while I held my knife and twisted it deeper into his chest. He was snarling and snapping his teeth but the fight was leaving him quickly.

He went limp and I fell back with great cat laying dead on top of me. I passed out.

I awoke to a great chill. I was shaking uncontrollably. The night had brought with it the first heavy frost of the year. My left leg was useless as I found out after rolling the stiff cat off of me. The leg did not seem to be broke but it was deeply bruised and swollen. I could not put weight on it. My scalp on the back of my head was loose and tattered. I had bite marks on my skull, arms, thigh and buttocks. I had scratches from head to toe and some serious deep ones at that. My shirt was in shreds and useless as a piece of clothing. Luckily I still had all my possibles , my rifle, knife and tomahawk. I gathered as best I could with my mangled hands the makings for a fire. It took a good hour with the flint and steel but finally I got a spark to catch in the small piece of birch punk I had in my haversack.

The fire warmed me some. I could hardly move and didn't really know what to do. I built up that fire and laid there in a hazy fog. Day turned into night and then into another day. I was cold. The fire wasn't cutting it. I crawled over the the big cat and it took me the whole day but I skinned him. I draped that skin over me that night as I roasted some of his ham over the fire and nibbled at it.

The next morning I was faced with a decision. I could crawl back to the shelter and lay up there until well enough to travel. If I did that I would miss the meeting with Chancy, he would set off looking for me and probably would not be able to locate the hidden camp. The other option was to take off for the camp in Tygart's valley. I could get there and we could return with the horses to pick up my pelts and other items.

I could not put weight on my leg so I built me a rough crutch. I wore the panther skin and started out. I made five hundred yards that day before collapsing beside a spring. I dug my fire makings out and my copper mug. I built a small fire and boiled water. I cleaned wounds I could reach. Then I boiled some panther meat and drank the broth slowly. My neck was swollen and sore.

The next morning I tried to get up to go but felt very ill. A fever was taking hold of me. I had always heard from my Ma that panthers and cats could kill you with infection from one scratch. I fell back on that panther skin and slept. The cold would not go away.

I awoke with a start to a cold drizzle and a fire that was out. I was shivering from cold and fever. I had to go, I had to make it to Chancy to even have a chance to get healed. I crawled that day. I don't know how far I made it but I found a small ledge with dry leaves and a rat nest under it. I got a fire going and built it up. I covered myself with the skin and soaked in the warmth. The next morning found a thick layer of frost on the ground and I crawled on.

My hands became bloody as did my legs. The fever was taking all strength from me. That evening I came to a creek and found willows and I hacked a bunch of bark and inner layer from them. I chewed the bark and made a hot tea from the rest. After an hour my fever subsided some. (Willow is full of "aspirin") As the fever subsided the realization that my wounds smelled of rotted meat started to worry me. I bathed them as best as I could reach.

I drank much hot willow tea and packed my bag full to carry with me. That afternoon I came upon a spruce tree that had been lightning struck. The scar was full of spruce gum. I melted this in my cup and filled my wounds with it. I also "glued" my scalp back in place. I crawled on and collapsed in a heap at dark against a log.

I awoke the next morning covered in sweat and still highly fevered. The willow tea was not taking the fever away as effectively as it was the last couple days. I crawled through a valley of large spruce and hemlocks that day. I came up a small clear stream. I casted a hand line in and caught a couple seven inch brook trout and devoured them raw. I crawled on.

That night I noticed the moon had started waxing towards full. I had to make the meeting with Chancy. I kept going. Each step was a chore. My arm was becoming wore raw from the crutch, the stench of infection was starting to nauseate me. I made a couple miles and collapsed. I built a fire with what strength I had. I slept in a ball around it with my body trying to pull in every bit of heat. The next morning I could not move. A stiffness had set in that was proving to be painfully impossible to work out of my joints. I tried to chew some jerky but could not hold it down.

I forced myself up and started out. Another couple miles and I collapsed again. I lay shivering under that cat skin with no fire.

The days ran together, the nights I looked at the moon. It was creeping ever closer to full. The fever was sapping all the strength I had. I could not hold down food or water. Now I started with the flux and I knew that soon I would be dead.

The next two days were a blur. My arm had an open sore wearing to the bone from the crutch. I had lost a good fifty pounds off of my one hundred and sixty pound frame. I had to get to that meeting with Chancy.

I laid that night by a fire, going in and out of delirium. I was in my mind enough to see that the moon was full.

The next morning I crossed the Middle Fork river. It was a small stream this high in the mountains. I tried bathing my infected wounds again. The flies had started on my back and I could feel the maggots squirming as they were eating my rotting flesh. I made myself continue on.

If I could only get to that clear stream I followed up from Tygart's valley. I would have at least a chance for my uncle to find me. I looked at that deerskin map and as much as I could tell I was still a dozen miles to the head of it. I headed on.

I collapsed at dark and built a fire. I could feel my lungs filling with liquid. I was starting to come down with pneumonia. I was dead for sure if that happened. I put together a fire and laid close.

Something started me awake! A wolf was pulling my leg trying to drag me from the fire! I swung my crutch and connected sending him yelping. Another raced in and grabbed the panther skin off my back. I cocked the .40 and fired. That wolf rolled over, kicked and fell still.

I grabbed a branch out of the fire and swung at the eyes of a third wolf and he backed off. The pack started circling warily as I reloaded and built up the fire. I started to surround myself with fires. I passed out in the center of them. I woke and built them back up with the wolves still circling.

Daylight came and the wolves had backed off. They were still lurking and watching me as I skinned their pack mate and added another layer to my panther skin.

I started on again. The wolves now keeping a watch on me as they shadowed my every move. I knew I had to get to that clear stream this day. I marched on through the delirium.

I collapsed that night again, my breathing rough and ragged. I was still at least four miles away from that stream. I had made the last ridge and where I collapsed was a worn trail. I passed out. My mind was telling me I was being eaten by a pack of wolves. I could feel them roughly tearing me apart. I could hear the wolves talking. Talking?

I opened my eyes to a focus and for the first time in days I was warm. I could see a fire. I passed out.

What I did not know was that a war party of Shawnee Indians had come upon my trail. They had found the dead wolf and continued following until they found me. I was being cared for.

When I woke the next morning, I was looking into eyes that seemed to be looking through me. " I am Hokolesqua, your people call me Cornstalk. What are you doing on Shawnee land?"

I explained to him that I was just hunting and passing through from the New River to Fort Pitt. My Uncle was somewhere nearby and would reward him for finding me and bringing him news of my incident.

Cornstalk sent two warriors then to find my uncle. For two days I laid in their camp while a sub chief named Wolf looked to my wounds. He had been busy making concoctions and packing the scratch marks on my back. He had also made a bitter tea with barks and a large fuzzy leaf plant. After drinking two cups of that I could feel a burning in my lungs. I started coughing and the fluid and mucus came out of them. The third day in their camp they built a small shelter out of canvass and put me in it. The two chiefs kept a fire with heated rocks going and then showed me how to pour water from a pot on the hot rocks making a heavy steam. They closed the canvass and I did as they instructed. I came out of there without the stiffness in my joints.

27

I started to hold food in also. I felt a little strength in me when Uncle Chancy came riding into the camp with the two warriors on the morning of the fourth day. He was pleased to see I was still alive. I quickly told him the story of the big cat. He just sat there shaking his head. Cornstalk and him talked the evening away. Chancy agreed to give them an extra knife and a French Fusil he carried on his mule as an extra weapon.

Cornstalk asked us to go to Fort Pitt and not come back into this area. That he would not kill hunters passing through as this land was given to all by the Great Spirit as a hunting ground. He warned us to take his word and warning and not to return. All Chancy would tell him was we were heading for Fort Pitt. With that they started on their way.

Chancy just shook his head when I told him the whole story. "Boy, you were walking dead and was lucky for sure. "He cared for me there in that camp for another three days.

The fourth morning it snowed. Chancy wanted to know if I felt like riding. He wanted to recover my furs and bee line it to Fort Pitt. I crawled in the saddle and held tight.

As we rode he told me that Cornstalk was calling me "Pounced on by a Cat". Chancy had shortened that down to "Catamount" and "Cat". We circled back into Laurel Run and stayed for several days at my rock shelter. Chancy added about a dozen more beaver to the pelt pile. I stayed in the shelter eating and resting. I was recuperating very well. After about three weeks I was up and at them again. Chancy had been feeding me bear and beaver meat. He said the fat would help me put weight on and heal up. My knee was not broke and it healed up nicely. I was ready for a long exhausting ride. Chancy wanted to head out before Cornstalk returned and caught us here.

We packed the pelts and hides up. We carefully packed all the ginseng root so as not to damage it. We headed out. We crossed to the valley of the Middle Fork and rode downstream. A couple days later we came once again to Tygart's River. We rode on down this river to where it emptied into the Monongahela River. From there we rode on and then stayed a night at the Decker's Creek settlement where Morgan Morgan had started his settlement.

We crossed from Virginia into Pennsylvania at some point. We followed the Monongahela the whole way. Just outside of Fort Pitt and the new settlement of Pittsburgh we joined onto the muddy road known as the Nemacolin trail or Braddock's Road. We crossed the battlefield still strewn with whitened bones and skulls of the Braddock massacre that occurred a short fifteen years before. 456 British soldiers and Colonial Militia were slaughtered by Puckshinwa and other chiefs of the Shawnee, Seneca, Delaware and other Great Lakes tribes. Chancy told me that even Braddock was killed but was shot by one of the colonials in the back. We were only nine miles from Fort Pitt.

28

Fort Pitt and Pittsburgh was the largest city I ever did see. Chancy took me to Alexander McKee's trading shop and introduced us. He beat me on few items, but I came out of there greatly stocked up for my next adventure. Some of the items I wanted was a wool blanket coat. Two additional large red wool blankets to make leggings and breechclout from. Some more leg traps for beaver was added to my larder. Also, tobacco, a pair of fine made lightweight calfskin boots. A heavy pair of winter moccasins. Some fur mittens and new Delaware pipe-hawk with a turtle design cut into the blade. I also made sure to get plenty of powder and lead.

We pulled out of Pittsburgh and followed Braddock's road back east. We reached a point where we cut south and came into the town of Romney.

We followed the South Branch of the Potomac all the way to the Rocks of the Seneca's. We then wound our way through the Spruce country as snow began to fill the mountains and the passes. We dropped once again into the Greenbrier valley. Here we came upon grisly scenes of Cornstalks slaughter. Cabins burnt out. Bodies still visible under the light snow cover.

We arrived in the valley of the New and closed in on my home. I, Jeremiah "Cat" Rogers was carrying the scars on my body but also the knowledge of an amazing land, filled with game, fur, land and pure water. I would be returning to the Middle Ground ....

" the Hunter "

30

Chapter 5
MOHONEGAN'S LAST HUNT

I have been on this western Virginia frontier now for twenty years. I have seen the changes in the red man, from the kindness of Logan the Mingo to the knowledge of Buckonghelas. The two chiefs have allowed men like me, Chancy Rogers, a chance to make a good living, hunting, trapping and digging ginseng. I have seen wonders in these mountains that cannot be explained. I have endured a war and several attacks by the French and their allies. What I have always done with these two chiefs is to respect and live with the land such as they do. I do not try to change them, I have learned how to live here from them.

The year is 1772 and the French-Indian war is passed. Britain has control of this part of the continent. The poor Scotch-Irish are flocking over the Allegheny front into this middle ground. All tribes recognize this area between the Allegheny front and the Ohio river as a hunting ground. Owned by none shared by all. The encroachment by settlers is starting to enrage the Shawnees. My friend Logan has declared a peace with all whites. My other friend Buckhonghelas has taken a new settlement on the Buckhannon River under his care and advisement.

Buckhonghelas and his son Mohonegan have taught that group how to plant the three sisters. Corn, beans and squash. How to catch and dry fish out of the river that shares the chiefs name. How to jerk deer and elk. How to make clothing grade leathers. They have taught them well.

I try to stay away from the settlements. Even though I am of their descent, I have been adopted into the native way and that's how I prefer to stay. There are to many whites that have pure hate for the red man. Jesse Hughes down on Hackers Creek is one. He is at the Buckhannon settlements a lot and no good will come of it. Up towards Wheeling you have The Wetzels. They hate Indians. These are the type of men that could make the frontier erupt at any minute.

On the other side of the river you have Cornstalk and Pucsinawah. Cornstalk has pushed for peace with the whites. Pucsinawah is the principle war chief of the Shawnees and he leads bands of young warriors up and down the Ohio terrorizing the settlers. I am stuck in between.

I do not have a home, I have never built more than a three-sided shelter. I have areas that I like to stay. I like staying out with my red brothers. I do make an occasional outing to Wheeling or Fort Pitt to sell my furs and pelts. I know I have to keep myself alert at all times because some white men do not trust me and some red men hate me because I am white.

This day finds me in Buckhonghelas' hunting camp on the Middle Fork river. Just a few miles from the settlement on the Buckhannon. We have a warm and dry three-sided shelter. It is a rock face with a that we have almost closed in with a hand laid rock fire reflector. Some of these mountain streams have good beaver populations and we are putting away pelts and meat for the winter.

I wear a grey and red wool breechclout with a Delaware turtle quilled upon it. I have a pair of grey wool leggings. I am wearing my winter stores since it is the Beaver moon and cold is settling in on the mountains. I wear a pair of center seam moccasins and with the cold and snow I wear a over moccasin type boot lined with beaver fur. These are heavily bear greased to keep water out. I wear a long hunter shirt of blue India print. Over this I have a heavy elkskin tunic. When the cold is brutal I have a french style capote made from two red British trade blankets. I wear fur mittens and a beaver cap covers my long hair this time of season.

I carry a faithful Maple stocked .40 caliber rifle that was made in the Susquehanna valley of Pennsylvania. I have a Scottish dirk with a stag horn handle. I traded a deserter of His Majesties Highlanders from Fort Pitt for this fine blade. I carry a ornate pipe hawk in my sash and belt.

I have a haversack and two possible bags with me. A wool blanket, a canvass sail piece, elkskin and a large bearskin make up my bedroll. I carry in my belt a new piece. A small .40 caliber pistol that I acquired on my last trading trip to Fort Pitt.

With this gear and possibles I can live quite comfortably all winter.

This cold still fall morning finds Mohonegan and me over watching a large chestnut flat. Buckhonghelas is making a quiet drive through a laurel patch.

We see glimpses of brown as the deer start coming our way. There are seven. I raise my rifle and wait for Mohonegan to fire. His trade musket doesn't have the range of my rifle. Mohonegan fires and a doe goes down. I pick out a young deer as it is bouncing away at 75 yards and gaining distance. I set the trigger and hold my breathing. The rifle fires. The ball travels 82 yards and hits the running Doe behind the front shoulder staggering her. Mohonegan and I immediately take off running out the ridge knowing that the deer always cross the ridge a good half mile away. There is a large buck in this group that would provide awls, knife handles, buttons for Buckhonghelas' wife and tribe.

As Mohonegan and I close in on the low gap, the five deer that are left are starting to cross the ridge. The large buck is last. We are still 120 yards away, but I have no choice but to raise and fire the .40 in one motion. The buck keeps running.

Mohonegan looks at me and says, "why you miss?" I set my rifle against a tree and yip and jump him. We roll down the hill in the cold snow wrestling and laughing. Buckhonghelas catches up. I reload and all three of us go to the spot the buck was when I fired. There are three brownish grey hairs in the snow. Two bounds later and there is red crimson blood on the snow. Just over the ridge is the finest and fatest nine-point buck that one could find in these mountains. We kneel and pray over the fine buck. I quickly then start skinning, deboning and making a pack while they Buckhonghelas and Mohonegan return to the other two deer to do the same.

Later at our camp while I am scraping the skins, Buckhonghelas looks across the fire and looks me in the eyes, "Chancy, I love you like my son Mohonegan, you are one of us. Where will you stand if these whites keep encroaching the middle ground?"

"Father, Buckhonghelas, I love my frontier father. You have taught me much. I love my brother Mohonegan and enjoy teaching him with you. I love my brothers the Delaware and the Mingoes, I will stand with you if there is war." I knew he would hold me to this and I meant every word.

"Father, this middle ground is meant for us all. There is room for us but the current settlements need to be as they are with no further encroachment, but I fear more and more of my race will stream over the mountains into these valleys. Running the deer, the elk and buffalo far away from here. This would not be good for us that live our lifestyle. "

Buckhonghelas and Mohonegan both shook their heads in agreement. I knew in my heart I was telling the full truth. I would stand with these two and the Delaware no matter what would come. I have come to love them both as father and brother. While we smoked and built up the fire for the night, Buckhonghelas said, " We should break this camp as soon as my braves arrive to take the dried meat back to the people. Then head to the Buckhannon river and meet with the settlers there for news and talk to Captain William White. Then we should trap the marshlands of Jawbone Creek for muskrat and beaver. "

I was uneasy about this suggestion. Many settlers were shooting first and asking questions later when it came to dealing with Indians or for that matter anyone that wasn't like themselves but I had to trust the chief. He knew William White and I did not.

Although apprehensive I was looking forward to the trip. Mohonegan had told me many times about a stream called Turkey Run that had many 500 pound plus bears roaming the chestnut bottoms of that stream. We definitely needed a couple large fat bears for the winter, we needed the fat meat and the grease. Also bear hides were always welcome as trade items or good warm winter clothing.

After a couple days, four Delaware warriors showed up by canoe to take our kills back downstream to the villages. We bade them goodbye then we headed out. It was only a twelve-mile trek to Bush's Fort on the Buckhannon.

As we neared I told Buckhonghelas and Mohonegan to hold back while I hailed the Fort in English and let them see I was white and friendly. I walked into the opening and boomed a "hail the Fort!!" To the top of my lungs. I was answered immediately. Once introductions were aside we were invited in and we were sitting and having dinner with the good captain and his wife.

William White looked in his late twenties, a few years younger than me. He along with eight families had come here to settle on the recommendation of John and Samuel Pringle.

Buckhonghelas had agreed that the families could live between the streams of Turkey Run and Jawbone but no further. Some settlers had paid this no mind and had bent the rules some by living at the Fort but making tomahawk claims from Hacker's creek in the north and French Creek in the south.

Buckhonghelas explained to the Captain that we would be bear hunting for a few days in Turkey Run then trapping the rest of the moon in Jawbone.

Captain White invited us to hunt bear with him as he had a good hound that was excellent at rousting the bears and even at times getting them to tree. We agreed.

That night I discharged and cleaned my rifle. As I reloaded I made sure to "load for bear". I upped my powder charge by twenty grains and after the first patched ball went down the barrel, I patched and slid another ball right on top of it. This gave the rifleman two projectiles. The first hitting 4 inches below the second ball. The second ball hitting where one was aiming.

The next morning the four of us headed to Turkey Run. The Captain loosed his dog a mile above the mouth. We had crossed a bear track in a chestnut bottom. Each of us being experienced hunters fanned out in different directions hoping to glance the bear and get a shot.

The hound was sounding off on a hillside I had headed for. He sounded as if he was heading right on my path. I was entering a laurel thicket when the brush in front of me started braking and parting. Out in front of me stood a 600 pound behemoth of bear. He had smelled me and stood for a look. I immediately took aim across the scant 45 feet and fired. The double balls struck the giant but not with the results I desired! He immediately dropped and roared as he charged with the hound right behind him.

I pulled the dirk just as the beast hit me full bore. It threw me and was on top of me instantly. The hound caught up and got his attention or the beast would have had my neck broke. As he turned to fight the hound I saw an opening and slammed the 11-inch blade in deep, I withdrew and repeated. The bear turned and swiped at me then collapsed in a pile on me!

Luckily the other 3 showed up immediately and helped me out.

The bear had survived one ball and two stabs directly to the heart. We discovered this while cleaning him and praying. Mohonegan built a small fire and cut the heart in strips. We ate the cooked heart there hoping to gain the strength of this fine beast.

We also cooked up some other fine cuts and got ready to head to the Fort. Even though I was cut up and bruised, I was no worse for the wear.

We hunted the next two days and killed three more bears. We shared with the settlers and made our way to Jawbone to make a camp.

After a full week of trapping many fine beaver and muskrats, Captain White made an appearance. He wanted to warn us that Jesse Hughes had cut tracks of a Shawnee band. They appeared to be hunting and tracking a group of British Army deserters that were staying on the head of the French Creek. We thanked him and continued with our trapping.

After another week, Buckhonghelas wanted to head to a great springs in the mountains where buffalo and elk frequented. (Modern Day Webster Springs on the Elk River)

We traveled up the Buckhannon, passing the mouth of the French Creek on up to where another stream entered. This Laurel Run was rumored to have some very savage panthers.

As we closed out the day we climbed to a nearby ridge and used the great Indian Camp rocks as our shelter. I took the first watch and settled in back away from here he fire staring into the darkness. All that warned me was a slight crunch on crusted snow. I immediately threw my blanket over the fire and yelled the Delaware word for attack!

The first brute to me was a strong-smelling fellow with mouth rot and red hair. He fired at me missing by inches, I pulled my pistol and shot him in the face. I side stepped his body and met the next one with my tomahawk. He had a short sword and swing at me. My tomahawk caught the sword and we held face to face. I was staring into the eyes of another white man. We came apart and I pulled my knife. I went at him and feinted with the tomahawk and drove the dirk through his chest.

The fighting had quieted behind me. I turned like a cat to see Buckhonghelas and Mohonegan bloodied but standing over the other two. We took our scalps and drug them away from the shelter. These must have been the deserters that Captain White had warned us about.

The next morning, we headed out towards the mineral spring. We did well and killed a buffalo and we dried several pounds of meat. I packed it up and carried it on my back. Buckhonghelas had our bedding and Mohonegan carried the extra weapons and supplies we took off the four English deserters. Mohonegan was sporting a new red coat of one of the deserters. It took us four days to get back to our Jawbone camp.

We each worked the buffalo robe and our new scalps. I took them just as my Indian brothers did. Twenty years before I would hesitate but now I know it's the way of the frontier.

The next day Mohonegan told us he was going to go to a little ridge a half mile away and try to get a deer or two with his bow. Off he went with his new red coat and his new trophy scalp hanging off his possible bag.

What a fine young man and a sight to see. This young man who I love as a brother would replace his father someday as a Delaware chief.

Buckhonghelas and I were wading a beaver pond in the Jawbone when a rifle cracked. We looked at each other and started on a quick run towards the ridge where Mohonegan was hunting with his bow. We knew he left his musket at the camp. We fanned out on this warm winter day. Most of the snow had melted off. We went forward tree to tree watching. Buckhonghelas let out the call of an owl. No response. We went forward another 100 paces and there sprawled next to a grape tangle in his new red coat was Mohonegan. Buckhonghelas and I ran forward, and the chief held his dying son in his arms on his lap. There was a hole where a rifle ball went through his stomach and had broken his back. The great hope of the Delaware tribe was bleeding out on his father's lap. Mohonegan could only whisper the word "white". Immediately we knew he was saying the name of our friend, Captain William White!

Mohonegan died right there and Buckhonghelas and I let out a death wail! We moved him out the ridge and dug a shallow grave. We lined it with bark and laid Mohonegan to rest with his bow and his possessions. (The grave is rumored to be under the site of the Upshur County, West Virginia courthouse)

Buckhonghelas looked at me and I shook my head yes. We started on the trail that took us right to Bush's Fort. Buckhonghelas called the Captain's name while staying out of range of the forts rifles.

Captain White came to the parapet. "Chief, I am sorry, I thought he was a Shawnee hunting me down! I shot before I knew. I never knew him to carry a white man's scalp and wear a red coat!"

Buckhonghelas voice boomed, " Captain White, you were my friend, you have murdered my son. I will hunt you down and will take my revenge on you. It may not be this night, but it will happen. I will kill you and take your scalp!"

Into the night Buckhonghelas and I went. A grieving father that was to be in the forefront of the middle ground burning and I, Chancy Rogers, am now in the middle of it!

"the Diplomat"

Chapter 6
BUCKHONGHELAS' REVENGE

1773, my rifle cracked and the Indian I was sighting on slumped over. I pulled my knife to go claim me a scalp. I got to the Indian and rolled him over with my moccasined foot. It was not just any Indian, it was Mohonegon, son of Buckhongehalas a good friend of mine and the settlers in this area. I had made a very deadly mistake.

My name is Captain William White, I am the leader of the settlers here in the Buckhannon River valley around Bush's Fort. We had gained permission from Buckhongehalas to settle and farm here. He had helped us establish corn fields and showed us hunting areas. Out of my haste I had shot the chiefs only son and had more than likely started a war.

I retreated quickly back to Bush's Fort and told Jesse Hughes what I had done. Old Jesse's advice was to "watch your hair".

That evening as the shadows settled in, we heard a booming voice outside the Fort. "White! It was the tracks of your feet that led away from my son. I will destroy this Fort and take your hair! It will not be today but soon! It will be soon!"

1774, the frontier here had been suffering increased hostilities. We had lived in peace until I shot Mohonegan. Now we lost some of our own. Just a few months ago John Fink had been slaughtered and scalped whilst he was boiling down maple sap. Now our good Governor of Virginia, Lord Dunmore, has put out a call for militia to go against the Indians.

Jesse Hughes and his brother had stopped by the Fort to see if I was going. We decided we would leave in the morning and cross the mountains to the Elk and float it down to the Great Kanawha and meet up with Andrew Lewis' army down that way.

We left out at daylight, we had not gone a quarter mile when we stopped dead in our tracts. There in the dirt of the cornfield was a defined track of a moccasined foot. Buckhongehalas was back. We all looked at each other and Jesse spat on the ground, "that red devil is going to cost me going to the war of the century!" I looked at those Hughes brothers and told them to go on without me. I would stay here and protect the settlers and try to get Buckhongehalas before he could do any mischief.

We all shook hands and they took off. I headed back to the Fort. When I was safely inside I explained what I had found to the others. I would have to go up the river and warm a few cabins. I took off. I blended quickly into the surrounding forest.

Buckhongehalas was not an idiot. I knew he had his eyes on me always. As I made my way through hillside covered in chestnut and oak towards the Pringle cabin I could just feel his presence! My hair was standing on the back of my neck.

I made it to Samuel's cabin without incident and rousted him and his wife and kids to head to the Fort. I then headed on out Jawbone Creek then to head to Finks cabin and get his son and widow to head over to Bush's.

A stick cracked, and I dove for a log. I cocked my rifle and started scanning the woods. All I saw was a squirrel a few yards away. The sweat had popped up on my brow and now a feeling of relief came over me. I started to roll over and get my feet when the arrow slammed into the top of my shoulder!

I was off like a deer! I got to the Fink's cabin and gathered them together and headed to The Fort. Once back there my wife removed that arrow and dressed the wound. Luckily it had only went through flesh on the top of my shoulder.

I scouted and hunted for Buckhongehalas or any Indian the next few days but did not see any or find any sign.

1776, Indian and British activity was picking up. The colonies had declared independence and the Brits were outfitting the savages with weapons in trade for scalps.

I was out a good ten miles from the Fort this cool morning hunting. Game was getting scarce within a mile of Bush's, so my hunting forays were ever expanding. I had traveled on horseback to the head of Slab Camp of the French Creek. I had already killed one deer with a good shot and was skinning and quartering it.

After finishing that job, I wanted to find a good fat bear. The Fort was getting low on bear grease. I tied up my horse in a low gap and eased out a ridge. I was snaking my way through some large cherry and poplar trees to a grove of white oaks I knew about. They should be dropping their acorns and the bears should be eating them. It was dry October day and cool. Just perfect. I made another quarter mile out the ridge hunting when in the dust in front of me was a small freshly built mound of dirt. There were two eagle feathers stuck in the dirt! Buckhongehalas was back and was here hunting me again!

I eased back towards my horse as quickly as I could go. My stomach was tight, and I was all beaded up in sweat. The old son of a bitch was a playing with me! I got back to the horse and started to swing up into the saddle when a shot rang out! The burning on my left calf let me know the old devil had winged me again! I took off running that mare as hard as I could.

I arrived back at the fort that evening. My lower leg crusted with blood and sore. My good Mary cleaned me up again. Her face as pale as can be. "We need to move a safer place, he's not going to give up until your dead or maimed!" I calmed her and assured her Buckhongehalas would tire of this game and leave soon.

1777, the savages keep hitting us hard. Not three months into the new year and we have lost two families already.

The sap was flowing, and it was sugar making time. We would take the sled out twice a day and collect sap in buckets. The oxen would pull the sled back to the Fort and the women would tend the fires and boil. The men would then go out and cut wood all afternoon for the next day's boil.

It was on one of these fire wood trips that Sam Pringle came running hard through the woods. "To arms, to arms! Redskins a coming! To the Fort!" We dropped what we're doing and all of us ran. We had just got in and barred the gate when the first screams and shots rang out. Bush's Fort was under attack.

I climbed up on the cat walk and looked out for a target. There two hundred yards away in the meadow towards the river stood old Buckhongehalas himself! The wind was picking up and a blanket that he had on was a flapping in the wind. The old chief was a stunning figure of a man.

We fired the rest of the day. We watched in dismay as the savages killed and roasted our oxen down at the maple grove. That night they started launching bear grease fire arrows into the fort. Luckily the weather was working against them.

We had held them off for a couple days when we came up with a plan to sneak young Jonathan Fink out and send him up the Turkey Run and drop down on Hackers Creek and make a run straight for old Jesse Hughes' fort and get us some relief. That night we dropped Jonathan off a wall on the backside where the Red Devils were not watching as vigilant.

The next morning revealed that we had sent for help just in time. About forty Indians leading a couple dozen horses rode into the clearing. I could make out the white renegades Simon Girty and Jeremiah Rogers as well as Blue Jacket and the Shawnee Chiksika. If Jesse did not get here soon with reinforcements Bush's Fort was going to be destroyed.

We exchanged shots throughout the day and that night the Indians gathered by the river around a huge fire. The drums started, and they danced. They were chanting something and finally I could make it out. They were chanting the name "Mohonegon" as they danced around the fire. Buckhongehalas had the whole Delaware and Shawnee nation ready to come down on me for the sin I had committed. The drums continued for hours then there was a pulsating scream and they rushed the fort! A heavy fire fight broke out.

The shooting slacked off after we repelled their advance. With an hour until dawn and their bon fire out, a silence settled into the valley.

Daylight showed us no Indians around. About an hour after daylight a group of fifteen frontiersmen led by Jesse Hughes showed up.

The Indians must of realized that back up for us was in the way and they left.

1779, it had been quiet since the siege some two years ago. We would lose a horse or cow now and then, but the loss of life had ceased around our Buckhannon settlement and Bush's Fort.

I decided to load up my horse and pack horse and head over the mountains to the Middle Fork river and hunt elk and trap for some beavers.

It was cold for November. A snow had been on the ground for a couple weeks, it seemed each night a fresh inch or two was added. Great tracking snow for Elk. I made a camp on the river's edge where the Devil's Run emptied into the river. I had a piece of canvass as a lean-to and built my fire up good. My camp was in some low branched hemlocks and rhododendrons not visible unless you were right on top of it.

The next morning, I climbed the mountain beside the camp. There was a meadow about three miles away and I wanted to check for Elk. As I closed on the meadow I could see several cows and calves moving around pawing for grass. I leveled off my .50 caliber Pennsylvania made rifle and held on the closest cow's neck. At the crack she was down. I quickly reloaded while the skittish Elk were sniffing the downed cow. I hurriedly sighted again and dropped a young spike bull that had moved close to investigate. He did not go far.

I skinned and quartered those two, I put the meat in each hide and made a sack. I took a length of cordage I brought along and pulled them up into a good tree out of reach of the wolves. I would come back in the morning and load these two up.

The next morning, I made a series of deadfalls and snares on the Middle Fork. I then took the horses and circled around a few miles to pick those two elk up. On the way I killed a large whitetail buck with an amazing crown of antlers as he tracked a doe through the snow-covered woods. I picked the elk up and headed to camp.

I checked my snares and traps and had two large beavers. After I skinned and had their meat on a spit over the fire I decided to cast a handline for trout. I caught twelve of the Brooke trout variety all two feet long. I gutted and split them and dried and smoked them over the fire. Mary would enjoy those.

The next morning there was an additional six inches of snow. I pulled my blanket coat tight around me. I walked the river bank checking my traps. I had leaned over and picked up a nice beaver as I stood up an arrow passed in front of face and stuck in the tree beside my head. I ran.

I made it back to the horses and quickly packed up and headed out of there to the fort. I did not tell Mary about that close call.

March 8, 1781 dawned a frosty cold. I picked up my rifle and headed out with a bucket, hand drill and several handmade maple taps. I had spent all winter carving taps from elderberry. I headed on to the maple grove and started my work. It took about four hundred taps in a couple

41

hundred trees to get enough sap to make our sugar for the year. We had made oak barrels as we now had a cooper that moved into our settlement. The sap would flow into oaken buckets and barrels. Our little settlement was growing now since the war for independence was over and it had been two years since an Indian had been spotted in our area.

I leaned my rifle up against a tree and bent over whilst a drilling a hole. I got two taps in and moved on to the next. This March Day was going to warm and melt the snow today. The sap should flow good.

I was drilling away, and I heard a slight shuffle behind me. As I turned a wooden balled war club smashed my left temple. I went to the snow in a heap. I couldn't get my eyesight to focus at all. A hand roughly grabbed my head and a slicing pain shot through my body as my scalp was removed with a popping sound. I tried to get up when the hand closed down on me and the next thing I felt was the knife blade cutting through my throat. My eyes cleared for a second, there stood Buckhongehalas with my hair. Scarlet blood sprayed on the snow. My poor Mary, then I was dead.

May 1805, I, Buckhongehalas am dying. I lay in my lodge in this Indiana territory far from the Middle Ground where my son lays in the ground. My life has been a struggle but has been long and good. I have sang my death song and I lay here looking into the rafters of my lodge. My prized possession is turning in a breeze. The scalp of White. It is the last thing I see as I go to the great spirit. I die with a smile on my face.

"Corn Planter"
A Joshua Sivan
9 - 2015

Chapter 7
FREEDOM

I heard the crack of the rifle and I dropped into the corn I was hoeing. I did not know where to go. Master had gone to the house to check on the Missus. When he went around the house that's when the rifles cracked. I was peering out and could see several Indians ransacking the farm. One big brave came running around the house with a bloody scalp of the master in his hand.

Two braves came to the cornfield and pointed at the ground. They figured out that someone else was in this corn field. My bare feet left different tracks than masters boots. The head warrior walked over, and they started looking for me. Finally, one saw me and said several words in amazement while pointing.

I stood up. I was four inches over six feet. I was wearing knee breeches and no shirt. These braves stared at me. They must never seen a giant black man before.

The head man walked up to me. "Speak English?" I nodded my head yes. "I am Cornstalk. You come with us. All dead here, you become Shawnee. "

That's how I got my freedom. Chief Cornstalk of the Shawnees freed me during a raid.

I was given a horse and fell in line with the braves. I was not given any weapons. I had only known this New River country since Master bought me from a trader in Richmond. We never had problems before with Indians.

We continued to ride down the New River. We passed the Gauley River and kept riding on a trail past a beautiful waterfall. That night we made camp along the Great Kanawha River. Cornstalk has told me the New and the Gauley came together to form this Kanawha. Cornstalk also asked me my name. "I am Caesar". Cornstalk looked at me and said some Shawnee words quickly over his shoulder. A brave brought me a musket, knife and tomahawk. "You will join us, you will be free. We attack the settlement known to whites as Kelley Creek settlement. You help, you prove yourself. You become a Shawnee."

I nodded my head and took the weapons. "You know how to use these? There are no slaves amongst my people. No one can own another."

The next morning dawned and we rode. When we closed in on this Kelley Creek we dismounted and stalked our way through the dew-covered grass. I stayed by the side of Cornstalk. He was painted a yellowish-white and I thought he looked brilliant in the morning sun.

We crawled close. A white man was carrying a bucket to the river. A couple other men and a boy were swinging axes into some trees nearby.

The Shawnee lept from cover with a scream. I followed Cornstalk. He took down a man with just a hard swing of his war club, half of the man's head disappeared. I pulled the tomahawk from my belt and followed Cornstalk to the river bank. We met the man there running back with the bucket and a knife in his hand.

He went under Cornstalk's swing and pushed him down in the brush. Then he stopped and stared at me. "Bad enough to fight savages now I got to fight niggers too!" I went at him with a roar and grabbed him with my left hand around his neck. I picked him completely off the ground and threw him. I then jumped on him and hit him three times with that tomahawk, killing him.

Cornstalk let out a loud trill, he motioned me over and drew his knife. He pulled the man's hair and with one swift cut and a popping sound he handed me the bloody scalp with a huge smile on his face. "You will be a mighty Shawnee warrior Caesar!"

We put the cabins to torch and mounted up. We rode to a ledge just above Campbell's Creek. Here we camped for the night. The warriors kept thumping me on the back and pointing at the scalp and smiling. One of the braves came to me and walked me to the creek. He cut my clothes off me and pointed to the creek. I waded in and while my back was turned he jumped me and pulled me in the water and pulled a hand full of sand off the bottom and started scrubbing me. When he finally let me out he threw a pair of moccasins at me, a long leather strap, some red cloth and a red silk scarf. I made myself a breechclout from that cloth and that silk scarf I tied around my head. The moccasins were a little tight but I wore them. I never had new shoes in my life. I walked back to the fire and the braves and Cornstalk hooted at my outfit. Another brave dug into a sack and pulled out a long shirt for me to wear.

The next morning found us mounted and riding. We turned and rode up the Elk River. 1766 the Elk was still wild, and we encountered no settlers. We crossed out of the valley of the Elk across a mountain and camped that night above a Creek that was lined with many cedar trees. (Cedar Creek, Braxton and Gilmer Counties).

It was here the next day that I shot a deer for the first time. I had snuck through a glade near the creek and saw the velvet buck browsing. I lifted the musket and broke his neck with the .69 caliber ball.

I was loving this life. I ate good. I laughed with other men. I was able to bathe when I wanted. I was not a black man to the Shawnees. I was a man.

We rode down the Cedar Creek to the Little Kanawha River. Four days later we rode to the bank of the great Ohio. Mercy I had never seen a river so big.

We swam the horses across and rode a trail up along the Muskingum River, we then rode across country and arrived three days later at Kispoko town.

The residents of this town gathered around and was staring at me. Some of the warriors came up and touched my arms. I noticed some of the women staring at me in admiration.

Another Chief came out of a lodge. He introduced himself as Puckshinwa, principal war chief of the Shawnee nation.

Cornstalk informed him that I was going to stay with him and he would be responsible to teach me how to be a Shawnee warrior.

I spent the next year with Puckshinwa and his family. He taught me the way of the Shawnee. About Moneto the creator and why the whites must be driven out of the Middle Ground.

The freedom I had! The places I was able to go. Puckshinwa and a group of four other warriors and myself rode west, we crossed river after river. Scioto, Mad, Maume, and Wabash. We rode for days. The woods gave way to Prairie.

Finally, after ten days of hard riding we arrived at the Mississippi, the grandmother of rivers. I had never seen a river so big.

We swam our horses across the great river the next morning. Once on the other side we cut north. Another day of hard riding and we came to the Missouri River.

Puckshinwa slapped me on the back and said that I was probably the first black man to see these sights.

For two weeks during the Strawberry moon we hunted buffalo. Stalking them in the rolling hills and also riding in amongst the shaggy beasts. We worked hard at skinning, scraping hides and jerking meat. Puckshinwa told stories of how Kentucky and the Middle Ground was full of Buffalo before the white man. That a man only had to ride a half day to find one.

We carefully bundled the meat and hides and prepared for the journey home. As for me, I was home. I was free.

Spring of 1767 came a little late. Puckshinwa was readying all of us warriors to attack the Settlements between Cheat and Savage Rivers and Redstone Fort. He also spoke in depth to me about being a warrior. How he was honored to have a good man like myself along.

We started out the next morning. I had come a long ways in two short years. My left ear I had pierced 7 times. I had silver rings in each hole. My nose had been pierced also and another silver hoop adorned my nose. I wore red wool leggings and breechclout. I also wore a long shirt and a green woolen frock. On top of this a Wyandot woman had made me a great coat from a couple bears I had killed. On my head I wore a red silk scarf. The bear coat had a hood with the skinned bear head attached. I was a magnificent sight to those around me. I carried a knife with a blade almost a foot long. I also had a Cherokee pipe hawk with a long handle tucked into my belt.

My rifle was a gift from Puckshinwa. He had captured this fine piece on a raid into Pennsylvania. It was a fine curly maple stocked .50 caliber rifle made near Lancaster. I also carried a small pistol. It was a smoothbore. I carried it loaded with a load of seven smaller balls. Very deadly when fired at twenty feet or closer. My possible bag was made from a wolf.

We crossed the Ohio north of the new town they were calling Wheeling. We crossed through some mountains full of magnificent timber. After another full day of riding we dropped into the valley of the Monongahela.

We crossed the river the next morning and followed an ancient trail that took us to the top of the Cheat Mountain. The Cheat River lay far below us in a canyon. This country was amazing.

The next morning, we took a trail to the bottom of the canyon and took another trail just above the river. This trail took us south as the Cheat ran north. That afternoon we came to a clearing along the river. A cabin sat on the far end. We tied the horses and advanced slowly.

We could hear noise from behind the cabin. We surprised a man that was sawing wood. Puckshinwa downed him with a strike from his tomahawk and then scalped him.

We broke into the cabin and no one else could be found. All the signs pointed to this man being a line hunter and trapper. We gathered everything up here that might be used and loaded up the horses. We continued.

We rode a trail up the next mountain and came to a place known as the Great Meadows. (Preston County, WV) There was a settlement of three houses and a mill, we rushed those and completely surprised them. We killed five men and boys and two women.

We took two women, one girl and two young boys hostage. This settlement had many fine horses and we helped ourselves. We loaded the prisoners up and headed on.

Another day brought us to the Savage river and here we burnt five different cabins. Killing another seven men and taking three more women and four boys prisoner. At this point we turned back and headed for Ohio country.

I talked at length with Puckshinwa about the nature of these raids. If they would ever stem the tide of the white man. I had grown up near Baltimore and had been taken to Philadelphia when I was younger. I told him there were more whites than could be counted. That for everyone we kill today, ten will come to live where the one was killed.

He told me that if anyone had to constantly live with the fear of death that they eventually give up and retreat. I did not see this the same. I could see a day when the whites would just come in droves with little fear. The whites believed themselves superior and ordained by their God to take what they wanted. Whether it was land or people.

47

We arrived back into Kispoko town. The prisoners were quickly doled out to families that had lost children or other loved ones. They would all be adopted into the tribe.

I lived with my Shawnee brothers for thirty years. My friend and mentor, Puckshinwa, was killed in 1774 at the Battle of Point Pleasant. I stayed associated with his family and watched his son Chiksika grow up to be a great and fierce warrior. His adopted son Blue Jacket became the Chief of all Shawnees after an adventurous life, filled with many victories and losses.

His other son Tecumseh would grow up and unite an Indian empire to stand against the advancing whites but that is a story for another day.

Then there was Caesar. Yes, I lived to be a ripe old age. I enjoyed every minute of freedom that I was given. From being born in chains near Baltimore to being a free Shawnee with a beautiful Wyandot wife. I have lived a good life, but I have seen the travesty that has occurred here with my brothers. Whites taking over their land and hunting ground. Murdering innocent hunters for sport. Raping and Murdering our women. I, Caesar have seen it all. I also cry for the loss of Kentucky and the Middle Ground with the realization that we will ever be herded west towards the Mississippi.

I am free, but am I?

"Making
Meat"

F Joshua Sims
6/15

Chapter 8
ESCAPE TO THE MIDDLE GROUND

The ginseng was thick like an emerald carpet on this steep hillside. I had spent the hot July day stopped over digging while always keeping a wary eye out for Indians or unscrupulous whites.

I don't think I will have many Indian problems. I am Chancy Rogers, blood brother to Logan the Mingo and Buckongehalas of the Delaware. The Shawnee that pass through can be friendly at times depending on their mood. If they are hunting and they see I am just passing through, I usually have no problems. There has been the occasion when some young warriors thought they would try me and that didn't turn out so well for them.

This area in western Virginia is known as the middle ground. It is an area of mountains full of game and streams full of fish that extend from the ridge of the Alleghenies to the Ohio river. This area is owned by none and claimed by many. It is an amazing place to call home. Buffalo, Elk and deer roam in amazing numbers. Turkeys are easy for the taking. Bears are on all the hillsides some of them weighing half as much as the huge buffalo bulls.

The year is 1769. The French-Indian war has ended, and the British have won control of the continent. Some of us don't set well with living the structured town life of the colonies. The religious fervor to be found in some of those towns can be downright restricting. That is why I left colonial Virginia years ago for this beautiful middle ground.

The Middle Ground is also that for my soul. It's a place where I cling to my Christian teachings while learning the way of red man. I have come to find out that his way of believing is not that far off from the way I was raised. It has helped me here to find a harmony and to live and learn from good friend like Logan and Buckhongehalas.

The ginseng I am digging will make its way back across the mountains to Colonel Washington's Mount Vernon. From there the good Colonel will grade it and it will be shipped to Cathay (China). I only try to dig the very large four and five prong plants. Some with roots as big as potatoes and necks with 100 plus years of growth buds on them.

On this trip in I had come with a young guy from the Yadkin valley of North Carolina. His name is Daniel Boone, he's a nice young guy and quiet. He wanted to dig six big barrels of the finest ginseng and float it up to Fort Pitt and then wagon it across to Philadelphia to be sold. I met him at a tavern on the New River and agreed to come show him around and help him.

50

We had canoed down the New to where the Gauley comes in and forms the great Kanawha. I helped him portage the falls, then told him about the Elk River and where it met with the Kanawha. He would take the canoe on down and establish a camp and dig the mountains up the Elk while I walked and dug from the Gauley over to the Elk.

These mountains were for those that were not faint of heart. Wild panthers, timber rattlesnakes, copperheads, bears and Shawnees was just a sampling of what could kill a man in this area.

As I climbed higher up the mountain and started traversing the country, I found patch after patch of ginseng. I had a long slender blacksmithed piece of iron with a flat end for digging. I would carefully remove each root, being careful not break any of the root off. My plan was to fill my canvass haversack full and meet up with Daniel in about three days' time. Since it is the warm time of the year I would be making dry camps and living off some smoked fish and biscuit I have in my kit.

Sometimes people have this misguided concept of what us frontiersmen looked like. Most picture is in fringed buckskin pants and jacket and fur hats made of raccoon. This could be furthest from true except during the very cold months. I had on a pair of doeskin leggings that came up right above my knee. They are tied off to my belt. I wear a doeskin breechclout with a quilled turtle on it. The turtle being a sign of the Delaware and I am brothers to Buckhongehalas. I wear center seam buffalo hide moccasins. My shirt is a very lightweight open front tea muslin. I keep a second belt around it that my knife and tomahawk hangs on. I have woven wool inkle belt leg ties around my leggings just below the knee.

On my head is a black beaver felt hat. I don't wear it all pinned up or as a tricorn. I like it wide brimmed to keep the rain and sun from my face and eyes.

I carry a large horn of powder and two bags. One is my possible bag made of Elk skin the other is a canvass bag. I also have a canvass back pack with me to carry the roots in.

My rifle is a work of art. It is a .40 caliber. The stock is a piece of curled maple. The butt plate, patch box and trigger guard are all fine German silver. My rifle is my life.

Daniel was outfitted like me. In fact, almost all of us frontiersmen in the Middle Ground took on the dress of the Indians because it was comfortable in this environment.

After three days of digging and walking, I had accumulated over a hundred pounds of roots. I had come down a big stream known as Campbell's Creek and I located Daniel's Camp just a mile or two downstream. Daniel had found several patches of ginseng and after I had emptied my pack into the barrels he only needed three more barrels to make his shipment.

As neither of us had eaten fresh meat in several days we decided to go look for a summer buck. We located a well-used trail coming to the river edge, we set up down wind and waited. Sure enough towards dark we heard the slight shuffling of hooves. Out stepped a beautiful velvet buck and started to drink.

We had agreed I would shoot and Daniel would stay loaded and watch my back. I took aim across the sixty yards and picked a deer fly that had lighted on the buck's neck as my target. I set the rear trigger and started to squeeze on the front trigger. The .40 jumped and the buck was planted in the mud. I quickly loaded, and we made it to the buck taking as much meat as we could back to our camp.

Daniel had decided to stay in this area and fill his remaining barrels and head to Fort Pitt hoping to get there before the Hunter's Moon. He would leave my portion of money with my brother John at his homestead on the New River near the North Carolina border. I was going to head up the Elk to a Big Sandy stream that flowed in and explore that country. We said our goodbyes and I headed out.

The country was unbelievable. It was as the Bible described the Garden of Eden. Huge fish of all kinds in every stream. Turtles that had shells three feet across sunning on the banks of the Elk. The shoals were filled with large freshwater mussels. Waterfowl everywhere. The mammals were even just as numerous, with the oak hillsides and chestnut ridges providing all the food that the beasts needed.

On my fifth day after leaving Daniel I had dropped into a stream known as Pigeon for the millions of passenger pigeons that roosted in the hemlocks upon its banks. I had made a camp back under a small ledge of rock and quickly was asleep. I was awakened suddenly by rough hands on my wrists and legs. I was jerked out from the ledge and was forced to stand. I was looking at one of the most magnificent Shawnee warriors I had ever met.

He was amazed that I knew his language. He introduced himself as Puckshinwa, principle war chief of the Shawnee nation and he wanted to know why I was in the Middle Ground against the treaties.

I tried to explain to him about my brotherhood with Logan and Buckhongehalas but he was having none of it. I was tied and led away.

As he led me away he was explaining to me how I should have stayed on the far side of the mountains. That for years us whites were pushing them little by little until now there are whites hunting Ohio country and Kentucky.

I trudged along wondering my fate. I kept watching for every opportunity to escape. As we walked miles up the Big Sandy to a point where the stream started to come down a narrow valley, we cut up on the mountain and hit a trail there. At night they would tie me to a tree in a manor so that I could not move. Puckshinwa explained to me that we were heading to the Little Kanawha river and would take some hidden canoes downstream to the Ohio.

Once to the canoes I was loosened and put to work. I think I impressed them with that ability. The miles went by quickly as we glided silently towards the Ohio River.

Close to the Ohio we passed a couple burned out cabins. Puckshinwa was telling me the story of how they had surprised and destroyed those cabins. They had killed two men, a young boy and two women. They took a third man and two young girls as prisoners. The girls had been sent to the Miami villages near Detroit and the man was awaiting his fate at Kispoko town.

We crossed the Ohio the next morning and began an over land trek. At night now, they were not tying me, I knew that they were daring me to escape. We walked another day when we were met by several young boys riding and leading horses. I knew we were getting close. Puckshinwa was riding beside me and talking the rest of the way. He wanted me to run the gauntlet and become a Shawnee. If I made the two-hundred-yard dash and surviving blows the whole way then I would be adopted. If I didn't make it I would be given two more tries. If I failed more than likely I would be burnt at the stake.

As we ride into Kispoko town everyone was gathering. As far as captives went, I was famous to them, I was right there behind Boone, Simon Butler and Lewis Wetzel. Capturing me really was a coup for Puckshinwa and his warriors.

Everyone started to gather in the large council house. I was led in and loosely tied to a support pole. A few yards away was another white man tied to another pole. He was painted black from head to toe. He was Cut-ta-ho-tha, condemned to the stake. His fate had been sealed.

As the council started many angry voices were heard. Accusations were swirling that I had killed many Shawnee and that I should be burned also. This was far from the truth. I had been in a couple scrapes from time to time with some misguided young braves, but I had never killed Shawnees just to kill.

Puckshinwa stood and quieted a crowd. He gave an impassioned speech about how I was brother to Logan and Buckhongehalas, that I had helped to push the French invaders out that allowed good trade with the British. He explained to them that I did not claim land and build cabins in the Middle Ground.

After his speech the consensus was that I was to run the gauntlet in the morning. If I completed it I would be adopted. The council broke up and the other prisoner and I was led outside. He was tied to pole with a five-foot strap from the pole to his wrists. He could walk around the pole.

I was tied to another pole 40 feet away with a view. The Shawnee stacked kindling wood all around the condemned man's pole in a circle about 8 feet from the pole. It was waist high when they finished. Then green saplings 20 feet long were laid around the fire so that only the point would burn.

The drums started beating and a warrior came out with a torch and lighted the wood. The pyre quickly caught. The poor settler inside

53

the ring started suffering immediately. He was fully surrounded by intense heat. The Shawnee knew what they were doing. The flames were not close enough to kill but were bubbling his skin and singeing his hair. The smell was sickening. The settler stumbled around the post screaming and praying. Every now and then a squaw or brave would run up and grab one of the twenty-foot-long saplings and jam the burning end into their victim.

This went on for an hour before the poor settler finally collapsed and died.

I knew I had to make my escape.

The next morning, I was brought to the hill below the council house, there were two lines of Shawnees on either side of the trail. I was approximately 200 yards from the council house. Puckshinwa told me that if I made it to the council house that I would be adopted. If I failed three times I would be burned at the stake that night. I eyeballed the long line and noticed that a warrior stood just outside the council house was leaning on my rifle talking with another Shawnee. He had my possible bag and horn hanging loosely on one shoulder.

Puckshinwa reached over and ripped my shirt and breechclout off. My leggings fell down to my knee ties and my moccasins were left on. Besides that, I was bare. The drum started beating in the council house about that time Puckshinwa slammed me across the back with his cane he had in his hands. I started up the line at a fierce pace. Most of the blows were missing me. I was close to the end when a warrior hit me with a war club a glancing blow off my temple and I went black.

When I came to I was back at the beginning. Puckshinwa asked me if I was ready to go again. I nodded. He helped me stand and before the drums and blows could start I took off. This caught the Shawnee by surprise. I was running up the gauntlet and no blows were connecting!

I got within sight of the brave with my rifle. He was still talking and not paying attention. I hit him full force and he went sprawling. I quickly grabbed my rifle and possibles and continued to run.

Being that I am 6'2 and long legged I put some distance between myself and my pursuit. Before they could get an organized party after me I had already gained a mile on them and was continuing. I also hoped to confuse them as I ran north by west, deeper into the Ohio country.

My plan was to run this way about twenty miles then cut due south. Hopeful to cross the Ohio and back into the Middle Ground or Kentucky.

Here I was a white man, wearing nothing but leggings and moccasins, carrying a rifle and bag with horn cutting through hostile Indian country. If someone was watching this from afar, I am sure they would have a good laugh.

After running most of the morning, I slowed and started taking inventory.

My rifle was in excellent condition. I had about 20 balls with me and plenty of powder. My flint and steel were still in my bag as was a small patch knife. A couple lengths of rawhide buck skin were balled up in there as well. I had plenty of tools to not only survive with but to thrive.

I started hiding my trail and watching how I walked. Careful not to crush grass or roll small stones. Many times, I would just run a fresh downed tree for its length and try every trick I knew to make my trail vanish.

After twenty miles or so I made my turn south. Kispoko town laid in the valley of the Scioto River. I had crossed a great area and hit Paint Creek. Paint flowed south and hit the Scioto River south of Kispoko town. I could then just follow it to the Ohio.

The next day I could just feel the pursuers close to me. It was sensed and felt more than seen. I had covered myself in a black mud concoction to help prevent mosquito bites and it also was warmed by the July sun on my skin.

I laid up in a bit of brush along a log and watched my back trail. Sure enough after an hour of quiet here come Puckshinwa and 2 warriors in my footsteps. They were walking my trail but had not found evidence of my passing. I let them pass and then I became the hunter.

I stole along the trail and kept them within my sight. That night they made a camp along the banks of the Scioto. They couldn't understand where I had gone to. Puckshinwa was saying they would continue to the Ohio and if I wasn't found they would return.

As they settled in, Puckshinwa and one of the braves fell asleep. The other moved out into the shadows to keep watch.

I slipped around the camp. I had no decent knife or tomahawk to attack with, so I was going to have to take this brave out, take his clothing, knife and tomahawk and get out without the other two knowing it.

I slipped in behind the brave. I slipped my arm around his neck and lifted him off the ground without a sound. I choked him unconscious. I did not kill him, but I did take his shirt, belt and breechclout also his knife and a very ornamental pipe hawk. I quickly continued down the trail.

Now I had on an India print longhunter shirt that hung down to my knees. A finely quilled Doe skin breechclout and a hand quilled belt tie. The knife was a red handled British trade knife and the pipe hawk.

It took three days more days of scrounging for grubs and edible plants and covering ground before I got to the Ohio. I looked around knowing my pursuers would be closing in. I quickly located a log and I lashed my rifle and possibles on top and pushed out into the current. I was barely fifty yards out when a shot rang out and a lead ball hit the log.

Puckshinwa was standing on the bank with his rifle smoking and smiling. "Brother! Do not go to the Middle Ground! Brother! I am going to hunt you and bring you back for the stake! Brother! Thank you for not killing my people! Brother! Do not sleep soundly in the Middle Ground!"

He was smiling great big as he bellowed these words out. As I gained my footing in the mud of the Kentucky side, I waved across the three quarters of a mile. Here stood two warriors only separated by water.

We both had deep respect for the other, but I would not listen to his advice. I started on the trail back to the Middle Ground and the areas I called my home.

Chapter 9
LOGAN'S FURY AND LAMENT

It was April 1774 when Logan, Chief of the Mingos and me, Chancy Rogers, were deep in the interior of the Middle Ground. We were looking at possible summer camp sites for Logans tribe. We had made it as far as the stream now known as Gandy and was looking over some old Seneca camps that had some carved baths below a waterfall. We had been here three days eating a buffalo calf I had killed the day before. We had feasted on the calf liver, heart and tounge. I had seasoned the dish with ramps and had picked a large mess of morels to eat also.

The next morning found us catching trout out of the creek. We then got down to the business of cutting some black alder to make some snowshoes as the high peaks of Spruce were still covered in several feet of snow. We wanted to drop into the valleys of the South Branch of the Potomac and scout some of the area from Seneca Rocks downstream for thirty miles to where the river went between two steep mountains. (The Trough between Moorefield and Romney)

It seemed every watershed we ventured up from the Ohio to the Allegheny spine was being populated by white settlers. Logan was disturbed by this but seemed to take it in stride. He had been at peace with the whites since the French-Indian war and had reaffirmed his peacefulness to The White Shawnee, Blue Jacket, before we left on this foray.

Blue Jacket told Logan that he had snuck up to a camp belonging to the surveyors Michael Cresap and George Rogers Clark (a distant cousin of mine) and heard the whites bragging that they would kill Logan and his family. Logan had listened kindly and then told Blue Jacket that he was at peace with the whites and the words were coming from loud bragging drunkards more than likely.

Blue Jacket had left with a warm handshake and a hug for Logan and told him to be careful. We had left the next day for this trek.

Logan had taken me in and adopted me as a brother. I had hunted and fought alongside of him for years in the Middle Ground. I had now been here over twenty years. I had recently escaped from the village of Puckshinwa, principal war chief of the Shawnees as I was running the gauntlet. After several months of the Shawnees hunting me I had made it back to Logan's camp on the Ohio at Yellow Creek. The Shawnees had then decided that I was an adopted Shawnee at the urging of Blue Jacket. The whole Shawnee nation saw me as a great warrior and friend

58

considering I had escaped and eluded them for months without injuring or killing any of their warriors that had pursued me.

Logan and I had just about finished our snowshoes when the spring birds went quiet. I grabbed my rifle and slid into the Rhododendrons and disappeared, I didn't have to worry about Logan as he did the same.

I slowly cocked my rifle and set the rear trigger. I was beginning to bear down on my sights as I picked up movement eighty yards out when the call of a barred owl rang out. Logan and I immediately answered it. We both stepped out into the open as a lithe Mingo warrior came up to us. We could tell he had been on the run for days looking for us as he was emaciated. We could also tell he was carrying bad news.

"Logan my Chief, I have come miles to tell you sad news of the death of your Father, Brother and Sister as well as ten of our bravest warriors."

From there the ghastly story came out. It appeared that the survey party has camped on the Ohio at Baker's Bottoms. Directly across the Ohio from the mouth of Yellow Creek. Shikellimus, Logan's Father had a camp on the river. A lone white man in a canoe came across and hailed the camp. He invited the Mingos across for a feast of venison and to drink some rum.

Shikellimus accepted. Soon thereafter a canoe carrying Shikellimus, Tay-la-nee, Logan's brother, 10 warriors and Logan's sister who was 7 months pregnant crossed over the Ohio to the camp. There they were met by a group of white men who had a deer roasting over a fire and were passing a jug of rum around.

Logan's brother and the warriors quickly were drunk. The white men had dug up some snapping turtle eggs earlier and had boiled them as appetizers. There were several left after the feast. A shooting contest had been contrived. 15 stakes had been driven in the ground at the distance of 20 paces and the the boiled eggs were set on the pegs. The drunk warriors and Tay-la-nee all took careful aim and fired. They were unsteady and were laughing pulling loading material out of their possible bags when Logan's sister screamed.

The whites took aim and killed 8 of the warriors in the first volley. They then clubbed Logan's sister unconscious and tomahawked his brother to death.

They tied Shikellimus to a tree. The white men then started taking scalps of the fallen warriors. They also took fingers, toes, penises and scrotums as trophies. They left the braves as piles of skinned meat.

They then turned their attention to the unconscious sister of Logan. They stripped her and three of the white men took turns raping her until she passed out again. Then the leader (later discovered to be Jacob Greathouse) bent a forked maple sapling over and stood Logan's sister up and put her head tightly between the forks, he allowed the sapling to spring up acting like a woodland gallows. It broke her neck. Greathouse then took his tomahawk and slammed it into her belly and pulled the seven-month-old fetus and entrails out and hung them all over the other saplings for the ravens and vultures to feast on.

Then he turned his attention to Shikellimus. Greathouse slammed his tomahawk into the old man's neck four times decapitating him. He then took the head and a twelve-foot-long cut and sharpened sapling and stuck the head on it and slammed it in the mud for all the Ohio river traffic to see. The party then took turns skinning off pieces of the old man to take and make wallets and bags out of.

Logan sat staring into space as the story from young man came forth. I, as a white man, was ashamed of my race and possibly the involvement of one of my cousins. As soon as the warrior stopped talking, Logan looked at me with a fierce look of hate in his eyes. "Chancy, you are white but my brother. I must now pick up the tomahawk and I will gain my vengeance by killing ten whites for every one of my family and tribe murdered! We must make haste and return to Yellow Creek to make council. I want to visit the site of this atrocity!"

I will give that young warrior credit. He had found us in five days of travel. He ate and was right with us as we took off. We crossed the mountains running. We crossed the valley of the Tygart and went up and over the mountain and dropped into the Buckhannon river valley. After a full day of running we camped on the banks of the river above Bush's Fort.

We started out the next morning before daylight startling the settles of the Fort as we ran through the meadow at daylight. We crossed over a couple small mountains and dropped into the valley of the West Fork river. We again crossed over three other mountains and smaller watersheds. After another night of a cold camp we continued on the run the next morning into the valley of Fish Creek that led us after another half days run to the banks of the Ohio. Up the Ohio we went to Baker's Bottoms.

There we were met with the ghastly sight. The warrior and I helped Logan to bury his family and warriors. We crossed the Ohio to Yellow Creek and camped there. Logan was very withdrawn that night.

The next day we made it to the village. Everyone was in a state of morning and had completely painted themselves in black paint. I stripped down and did the same. No food was served, and no council was called for three days.

As I sat in a lodge loaned to me I searched my heart. I had reached a point where I could no longer exist as a middle person in the Middle Ground. I had seen that the Indian just wanted to live and have families and provide for themselves, but the intrusion of my race was starting to make this impossible. Even peaceful Natives such as the Mingos could no longer live in peace. The outer fringe of white society was eating away at the very existence of my red brothers.

I, Chancy Rogers, could no longer be torn between two lives.

60

The drumbeats were pulsating and the post in the center of the village was painted red. Logan and his braves had not seen me for the three days of morning and fasting. I waited until I could peer out and see Logan leading the war dance. I quietly made my way to the edge of the firelight. I had on a grey wool blanket draped over my head and completely covering me and when I dropped it the rest of the village and the dancing warriors paused and stared. I had plucked and shaved every hair off my white body except a scalplock I left on the back of my head. I stood there naked painted red from head to toe. The only clothing, I wore was my center seam moccasins. I help my pipe hawk in my right hand and when my blanket hit the ground I lifted my hawk above my head and let out such a primal scream that some of the women stepped back. My scream was met by an equally viscous scream by all that were there!

With a quick nod by Logan the drums started again, and I joined in the dance. As I lost myself in the beat, the drums quickened as we circled that post, swinging our tomahawks into the air at imaginary enemies, some had war clubs and would take out a white man in their trance.

I had danced and worked myself into such a frenzy that I jumped at the red war post and with a scream I slammed my tomahawk into it, I was startled to see blood splatter everywhere!

The dancing continued all night.

The next morning Logan, myself and the warriors all gathered. He drew in the dust his plan. For the next two moons he wanted hit every homestead he could from the Monongahela River valley to the valley of the Kanawha and New. He wanted to only attack cabins to wipe out settlers. No forts. We broke into two parties and headed out. Logan's war had begun.

When we hit the trail, I had my .40 caliber rifle. It had a maple stock and was a good Pennsylvania rifle. I wore new doeskin leggings and a breechclout. My waist ties and legging ties were handwoven and were bright blue, red and gold. I had a walnut stained linen shirt that hung to my knees. In my belt was my Scottish dirk and my pipehawk. I carried a deerskin possible bag and powder horn and a canvass bag on the other shoulder.

We traveled light and was planning on living off the land while out.

Our group of 15 headed across the Ohio and made our way back to Fish Creek, up Fish Creek to its head and we crossed three mountains and slowly dropped into the Monongahela River Valley. Here we encountered our first cabin. It was a new homestead on the river bank about halfway between Zaquil Morgan's town and Jacob Prickett's Fort. We watched the cabin for over an hour that morning, waiting.

A man and a small boy went towards a clearing with an axe. Logan gave the orders for half to get the man and boy and the other half to take the cabin. Logan's orders were simple. No torturing victims, kill them. Ransack the cabin for useable values and then put it to the torch and move out.

I moved with the group to the clearing. The axe was ringing as the settler was striking the great tree. I motioned to the warriors to be ready

61

that I was going to shoot.

I took careful aim over 60 yards distance and pulled the trigger. The sound of the shot was still echoing on the mountains when the warriors screamed and attacked. The little boy was clubbed and was down. I grabbed my dirk and took the man's red-haired scalp.

I looked at the cabin and saw that the Logan and his warriors had two long haired scalps in their hands and were already carrying off several items from the cabin.

We torched what was left and headed up the trail. One of the braves was the proud new owner of a very fine walnut stocked rifle. Looked to be .45 caliber. We had killed a man his wife, young son and a teenage girl.

We continued up the Monongahela and attacked every cabin in this manner. We burnt out three more before reaching Prickett's Fort. Here we cut across country to avoid the Fort.

After skirting the Fort, we came upon two more cabins and killed all there including a two year old toddler. We came to the West Fork and headed up river here. The plan was to go to the head of the West Fork and meet up with the other group of warriors as they came up the Little Kanawha Valley.

A good twenty miles up the West Fork we attacked and decimated several cabins around the Shinn's town. Here we gained several more rifles for the warriors. Soon everyone would be outfitted with quality rifles. So far we had no resistance.

The next group of cabins was in an uproar as we approached. There were three built together with a blockhouse at the mouth of Hacker's Creek. We could tell they had heard of what was going on. Defenses were being built. We tried to attack and was driven back. We lost one young brave from a round ball to his forehead. Someone in the blockhouse could shoot!

We surrounded and fired into the cabins. I kept hearing someone swearing at us. After a few hours a white flag showed, and Logan ordered everyone but me to stay hidden. Logan and I approached the Blockhouse. As we got closer I could see it was Jesse Hughes. Jesse was a Indian murderer and Logan and I both knew this. I kept him covered with my rifle lest he pull some sort of treachery. Jesse was also rumored not to be of sound mind which also made him unpredictable in battle and dealings with him.

Jesse wanted to know what was going on and why Logan was on the warpath. I explained to him quickly and that if they surrendered and the cabins burnt, livestock slaughtered, and weapons turned over, Logan would give this group quarter as long as they headed back to Fort Pitt or over the mountains out of the Middle Ground.

Jesse scratched his face while listening and after Logan finished talking he looked at me and Logan and said, " I reckon ye can go to hell, we will fight. Rogers if I can I will shoot ye and if I cannot I will scalp ye one night in ye sleep."

With a nod from myself to Jesse we retreated.

The gun fire resumed. Logan came to me and thought we should pull out before this small siege alerted even more settlers. I agreed but didn't like the thought of having old Hughes on our back trail. So we agreed to leave the West Fork valley and cut over the mountains to the Buckhannon River valley then to the head of the Little Kanawha.

We backed out and headed over the mountains overlooking Hackers Creek, dropping into the Buckhannon River valley where the Pringle brothers had stayed in the tree. We skirted Bush's Fort and cane young a John Fink working in his corn field. We quickly killed and scalped him taking his horse for a pack animal.

We headed up the Buckhannon and attacked a family on French Creek, killing six and burning the cabin. We crossed over the mountain here onto the head of the Little Kanawha.

After two days here, the other party showed. They had lost no warriors and had forty-three scalps. They had destroyed eleven cabins.

So, we moved on sweeping into the valley of the Elk River destroying a large hunting party at the mineral springs on the Elk. (Webster Springs). We crossed the mountains and dropped into the Greenbrier River valley, methodically destroying every cabin in our way. We avoided the area of Andrew Lewis's well-fortified Fort and made our way down stream to the New River. Between the Gauley and the Elk River we destroyed another 6 cabins. Killing another twenty-one whites and one black slave.

Every day was filled with slaughter, fire and smoke. The Middle Ground was burning with Logan's Fury.

After making our way down the long Kanawha River valley and destroying another nine homesteads we came to the Ohio River. We had been out two moons and had one hundred nineteen scalps amongst us. It was here at the mouth of the Kanawha that Logan decided we should head North and back to the Yellow Creek Village over a hundred river miles up the Ohio. Unbeknownst to our group, the story of Logan had spread to the Shawnees and the Delawares and they were at the same time attacking settlements and laying siege to forts at Wheeling and all through the Middle Ground. 1774 almost became the summer that the whites were driven back to over the mountains. Cabins lay empty and desolate and the few hardy souls that stayed in the forts were the only ones to survive Logan's war.

After several days on the Ohio we finally crossed and went up Yellow Creek. Logan decided to strike this village and move further into the Ohio interior. There he made camp at the village of Buckhongehalas. Here Logan built a cabin and lived out his life in silence and despair, falling to the rum bottle and murdered by a family member in the end.

That October, after the Battle of Point Pleasant, which is a story for another day, Colonel Andrew Lewis and Governor Lord Dunmore marched their armies onto the plains in Ohio within sight of several Shawnee,

Delaware and Mingo villages. Dunmore made camp and named it Camp Charlotte. Chief Cornstalk sued for a peace treaty and got it. The Treaty of Camp Charlotte moved the new treaty line from the spine of the Allegheny Mountains to the Ohio River.

Logan had been sent an invitation to attend and to sign the treaty. Instead he sent a speech by letter to those assembled.

"I appeal to any white man to say, if ever he entered Logan's cabin hungry, and he gave him not meat; if ever he came cold and naked, and he clothed him not. During the last long and bloody war, Logan remained idle in his cabin, an advocate for peace. Such was my love for the whites, that my countrymen pointed as they passed, and said, Logan is the friend of white men. I had even thought to have lived with you, but for the injuries of one man. Col. Cresap, the last spring, in cold blood, and unprovoked, murdered all the relations of Logan, not sparing even my women and children. There runs not a drop of my blood in the veins of any living creature. This called on me for revenge. I have sought it: I have killed many: I have fully glutted my vengeance. For my country, I rejoice at the beams of peace. But do not harbor a thought that mine is the joy of fear. Logan never felt fear. He will not turn on his heel to save his life. Who is there to mourn for Logan? Not one."

The Middle Ground borders had been pushed further West again. I could not go back to being white, I was now part of the ongoing war against the whites. Where would it end? What would become of a white warrior such as myself?

F Joshua Simons
6/2015

Chapter 10
BATTLE OF POINT PLEASANT

The frenzy of war was all over the middle ground! Logan the Mingo, long friends with the white man had declared a war after a group of whites led by Greathouse, tricked his family into a shooting match. Once the Mingos rifles were empty the whites shot down the Mingos. The men were all butchered and scalped. Fingers, toes and penises taken as trophies. Logan's own sister, six months pregnant was hung in a tree, killed and disemboweled. Her baby hanging from a sapling, dangling there lifeless among the intestines and gore.

Upon the discovery of this Logan declared his revenge. He was going to take ten white scalps for every killed member of his family and he did with brutal efficiency.

Logan and his braves roamed the countryside from Fort Pitt in the north to the New and Kanawha River Valleys in the south. They killed every white that was encountered.

This atrocity and Logan's revenge also stoked the fires of the Shawnees. Groups of Shawnee braves stalked the settlers from Lake Erie to Kentucky.

Governor Lord Dunmore of Virginia upon hearing the cries of the citizenry had raised two armies. One that he commanded that would float down the Ohio from Fort Pitt and meet up with Colonel Andrew Lewis and his force of about a thousand men on the Hocking River. Together the armies would sweep into the Ohio country and destroy the Shawnee, Delaware and Mingo villages.

October 1774 was going to be a bloody month. I am Jeremiah "Cat" Rogers. I came to these villages searching for my sister after my family was slaughtered by these Shawnees and my sister taken. I found my sister and I also found a life that I wanted to live. (The story of Jeremiah Rogers will be released in the full frontier novel TISKELWAH, coming soon) I became friends with Puckshinwa the principle war chief of the Shawnee Nation. He took me in like a son and taught me so much. So now here I am in Kispoko town of the Shawnee awaiting the war council.

I have come to accept that the Shawnees and other native tribes were correct in their standing. The great Creator had given them this land. My race was trying to take it. This was the home of the red man since the beginning.

I knew where I stood. I would fight with my Shawnee brothers against my own race. The only conflict inside me was that of religion. I had come to believe that the God I grew up with and Moneto that Puckshinwa taught me about had to be the same. I had formed my own hybrid belief and was trying to come to an easing of my heart over these beliefs.

My uncle, Chancy Rogers, had been like me. He had lived in the Middle Ground for twenty years. He was blood brothers with Logan and Buckhonghelas of the Delawares. He had fought with them against red and white man alike. I guess I was cut from his image more so than my own timid farming father.

The war council started. Puckshinwa gave an impassioned speech that fired the braves and the old men. The crowd was in a frenzy for bloodletting! Then Cornstalk, principle chief of all the Shawnee gave just as much of an impassioned plea for peace. It did not go over well and the tribe overwhelmingly voted for war.

The next step would be the women's council. If they voted no on war, then there would be no war. The next day, us men sat around cleaning weapons, measuring powder and molding round balls. Puckshinwa made a speech to the women and left. Nonhelema, warrior sister of Cornstalk, made an impassioned plea on behalf of Moneto and Jesus Christ not to go to war. She was a converted Jesus Indian by Moravian missionaries. In the end, the women voted to destroy this white army.

Chief Cornstalk, while disappointed agreed to lead the Shawnees into battle and the planning started.

As the drums beat into the night and the warriors danced the night away around the red painted war post, I gathered my belongings together for the fight. Cornstalk had decided to attack Colonel Andrew Lewis' force. They were marching from the Greenbrier valley, down the New and Kanawha. They would be exhausted and more than likely stop on the western Virginia side of the Ohio to rest. Shawnee scouts had picked up the army's scout trail. They had followed them to a point where an advance camp had been made. This point, Tu-Endie-Wei, was a perfect ambush site if the army camped where the scouts did. The great Kanawha river flowed into the Ohio here. The other flank was a deep banked creek called Crooked creek. The Shawnees, Delawares and Mingos would take canoes across and slip down into position, while some others would go down and up the Kanawha. Then a battle line would be formed, and the warriors would try to push the white men into the two great rivers.

Our force was numbered at about a thousand warriors as was the Lewis army.

I kept gathering my things together. I had been involved in several attacks and had killed my fair share of Indians and white frontier scoundrels, but this was to be the first pitched battle I ever took part in.

I carried a fine rifle of .45 caliber. It was handcrafted by a rifle maker in the King Mountain vicinity of North Carolina. The stick being full beautiful walnut and the iron forged pieces just blending well into the darkness of the wood.

In my belt would be a large scalping knife, a simple forged tomahawk and a matching .45 caliber pistol.

I carry a buffalo hide possible bag and a horn of powder. I am wearing a set of heavy buckskin leggings and a buckskin breechclout. A muslin open front shirt that I keep tied with a bright red woven wool belt. I wear a center seam style moccasin. I have a wool blanket cape with a heavy wolf skin attached to it for added warmth and some shock value. Puckshinwa has me to paint my face a pasty yellowish-white.

As we make our way to the camp on the Ohio, the unknown to me is stressful. Will I be able to stand up and fight in a pitched battle against my own race? Will I be able to kill men that are related to me? That believe in a God that I fully followed at one time?

After a partial night on the banks of the Ohio in a cold camp, we load the canoes. With fifty canoes holding up to ten warriors each, it takes a couple trips to get all of us into place. Having lived with the Shawnee now for more than a year I was used to the garishly painted faces. Puckshinwa had painted his face half red and half black. He had foreseen his death this day in a dream last night.

He led me, his oldest son Chiksika and another white youth that was called Blue Jacket into position.

Cornstalk, his brother Silverheels and his great warrior sister were taking over different sections of line. We crept forward inches at a time creating a tight line of red men across this peninsula.

As the morning fog was setting into every low spot of earth and the chill in the air reminded us all that the Hunters moon was upon us a shot rang out as a white hunter had seen a warrior as he was making his way to the camp. The cry of "indians!!!!" arose from the camp. Colonel Andrew Lewis could be heard bellowing "To Arms, To Arms!"

I took careful aim down my long rifle and a slight hesitation I fired. I saw a man tumble then the war cries, rifle fire and screams of agony numbed my mind and I charged. In front of me rose a man in a tricorn officers hat and I fired my pistol into him as he fell I saw a chubby greasy frontiersman squatting emptying his bowels and crying. I swiftly swung my tomahawk into his temple and the whimpering stopped.

I went into a crouch and looked for another target. I saw Silverheels take a ball through a shoulder and go down. The Virginians were starting to form a line and were firing with accuracy and furry. I saw a militia man in a beechnut colored frock taking the scalp of a warrior. I ran at him and he turned in time to meet me face to face. I swung my hawk at full force and as he blocked it with his knife and rifle, as My momentum to me past him I slammed my knife into the back of his ham pulling up as I stabbed. He went down in pain screaming as I hit him in the chest with my tomahawk.

The firing from the Virginians was intense so I backed out and laid behind a log with two of my brothers. I reloaded my rifle and pistol and started returning fire. The Shawnees had reformed their line and were doing the same. We were starting to make them wane. A couple times the Virginians made a push which was met by us.

The second time they tried this I locked into hand to hand combat with ole Jesse Hughes from up on the West Fork and the Buckhannon. We went toe to toe until each was exhausted. We both backed off from each other to our respective lines.

The acrid blackpowder smoke was amazing! It hung in the fog and well after the fog burnt off the smoke remained. This hand to hand fighting and firing from lines went well into the afternoon.

Just a little after the high sun of noon I spied an officer getting a group of men together to rush our line and try to break out. I sighted down my rifle and even though the range was great, close to 200 yards, I set my rear trigger and touched my front one. My ball traveled the distance and struck the officer in the forehead, killing him instantly. That officer was Colonel Charles Lewis, brother to Andrew Lewis. (Lewis County, West Virginia would later be named in his honor)

The intense fire continued, and the Indian line started to waver. We backed up a good fifty yards. Cornstalk could be heard all over the battlefield encouraging us to fight and hold and advance.

Puckshinwa was a demon. He had killed and scalped several militia men. He was encouraging our section of the line to make another advance. As he raised to go a ball struck him in the chest, slamming him back and draining his life. Chiksika and Blue Jacket carried him to a canoe.

Within a couple hours Lieutenant Isaac Shelby and about 40 of the Virginians made a flanking maneuver on our right on Crooked Creek. Cornstalk thought that this was reinforcements arrive from Lord Dunmore's army and he called for a retreat.

As our canoes crossed back into Campaign Creek on the Ohio side, I did not know what the future was to hold for me a renegade white in the Middle Ground. I would be forever a marked man like the Girty brothers. Hunted and disdained by the Virginia settlers.

Our losses were minimal, but we had lost our war chief and my adopted father. The militia losses were much greater, yet the battle could not be called a win by either side.

With a cold winter before us the future was uncertain as a new period of unrest and fighting started in the Middle Ground.

Chapter 11
BLOODY YEAR OF THE THREE SEVENS

The war drums were sounding a constant beat. Garishly painted warriors were dancing around the red painted war post. The Shawnees were preparing for war. The year is 1777. The year of the three sevens. There is a revolution raging on the eastern seaboard. The thirteen colonies are trying to break from the King of England. On the western front George Rogers Clark and his "army" of what same say was less than two hundred men have captured the Mississippi River valley from the Ohio River to north of the Missouri River.

General Hamilton, commander of the Fort at Detroit has been buying scalps and providing the Shawnees, Delewares, Miamis, Weas and Mingos with lead, powder, quality trade muskets, wool blankets, tomahawks and the red handles scalping Knives by the thousands. The General is encouraging all the Indians to attack the settlers from the Ohio to the Allegheny Mountains. To slaughter and pillage and to bring him the scalps and prisoners. While Hamilton says to bring the women and children alive to him, these are empty words because he still buys any scalp that is brought to Detroit.

I am Jeremiah "Cat" Rogers and I have come to live among the Shawnees as an adopted son. I have been given a homestead area by Buckhongehalas of the Delawares on the Big Sandy Creek that flows into the Elk River but with the intrusion of more and more settlers, families have moved onto my home site and have begin hacking the timber down and planting crops. I have been staying most of this winter in the Ohio country, making frequent trips to Detroit with some of the prominent warriors.

This night finds the war dance happening because Chiksika, son of Puckshinwa my adopted father and Blue Jacket another adopted white and I had recently gained permission through a war council to attack settlers in the Middle Ground.

Our plan was to strike up the Little Kanawha River to the Hughes River following it all the way to its head then crossing over a single mountain and dropping into my valley on the Big Sandy Creek. We would try to wipe out the settlers in that area. Then we would cut overland attacking settlements on the Elk River cutting across the mountains to the headwaters of the Little Kanawha and into the Buckhannon River valley. There we would try to wipe out Bush's Fort and the settlers in the surrounding countryside.

In two moons from now Chief Buckhongehalas of the Delaware's would begin the attack on Bush's as he had a blood vengeance with the settlers in that area. Captain William White that oversaw settlement and construction in that area had killed the chiefs only son, Mohonegan, after the chief had friended the whites and had given them permission to use the valley.

The war planning had gone on for days with visits from Alexander McKee, British Agent and Officer and the Girty Brothers, White renegades such as we were branded in that day.

McKee had approached me and Blue Jacket and had talked about our white ancestry. I had no problem with this, but Blue Jacket would only respond that he was a Shawnee and that white blood did not exist in him. McKee asked if I would keep extensive notes in a journal he provided to me. He reminded me that the King would be rewarding those that served the crowns interest well with land after this war was over.

As the drums continued throughout the night I readied myself for the upcoming trip. I made sure I had plenty of powder and lead. I took two horns of powder on this trip. My larger horn having the area of the Buckhannon River valley and the Little Kanawha River valley carved into it for reference. I packed all the extras I might need into my canvass haversack. Checked out my deerskin possible bag to make sure I had plenty of balls, patching and small pack of tools to work on broken rifles. I carried 10 extra flints with me also.

My knife was sharpened to a real fine hone. I put an edge on my simple tomahawk.

My rifle was made in North Carolina and is a .45 caliber. It's walnut stock and forged iron parts just complement each other. I have lived with this rifle in my hands since my father gave it to me when I turned 12 and I could barely carry it. I could shoot a turkey gobbler in the eye at fifty paces with ease.

My dress is simple. I wear a deerskin breechclout, deerskin leggings that come up just above my knee and center seam moccasins made from Elk. I wear a linen longhunters shirt and a deerskin tunic over this. I have plucked and shaved my head so that I have a scalp lock on the back. I look to be Shawnee.

The sunrise was crisp and cold as we left. The influx of stolen horses from the Kentucky settlements allowed us to go horseback. We planned on moving swiftly and quick. The Ohio was slightly swollen with the spring thaw but had not reached the muddy torrent it would be in a few weeks when the snow melt made its way from the mountains. We crossed with no problems. We rode on the ridges above the Little Kanawha that only the natives knew. Trails worn down by centuries of mocccasined feet padding through on them.

We crossed the Little Kanawha and headed up another ridge system to where we were overlooking the Hughes river. The nights were cold when we camped but the days were warming. The women back at camp would be making maple sugar now to get a sugar supply for the year.

We were skirting homesteads and small settlements. Our plan this time was to start on the interior of the Middle Ground and roll the settlers back towards the Ohio. We were not the only party out. Buckhongehalas was leading strikes in the north. Chiksika here with us. There were other parties making strike and go thrusts up the great Kanawha and on down into Kentucky. This year would be the Shawnees and other tribes last best chance at re-establishing the Allegheny mountains as a dividing line between red and white.

We finally arrived at a ridge above where I had been given land by Buckhongehalas to farm and live. Several families had encroached into this country on the Big Sandy Creek. White men had taken this land and cleared out the forest and were putting cornfields along the creek. One family had even built a small cabin on a stream that I had name Rogers's Fork and had tomahawk chopped a claim to such. It was not the pristine valley it had been just a short three years ago.

We made our plans. The strongest cabin was built at a mouth of a stream that came from the very ridge we were sitting on. (Presently where the WVDNR office sits on Wallback Wildlife Management Area). This cabin, owned by William Cookman, was built as a stronghold for other settlers to come to. It had one blockhouse built into it for defense. Little did we know Cookman had left to join the continental army and his seventeen-year-old son was running the homestead.

We made plans to break into groups of three and attack the other small outlying cabins. I took two warriors and we headed to the cabin on Rogers' Fork. We made our way silently down the hillside.

We could hear voices in a stand of sugar trees. A man two boys were drilling the maples. We watched as they worked and watched the cabin.

After about an hour a lone woman came out and shielded her eyes and looked up on the hillside. When she went back in we started moving. One warrior headed for the cabin. The other and I headed for the men and boys.

The man had leaned his rifle up against a tree and was several yards away. They didn't have any other weapons visible. We crept into range and with a scream and a shot we were upon them. The man went down from the first shot. A warrior was upon him and taking his scalp. I was facing a large boy of about fifteen that had a large wooden mallet in his hands. As I closed the distance he swung. I went under the clumsy swing and struck him in the back of the head with my tomahawk, killing him instantly. I quickly took his scalp as the third warrior was chasing down and killing the second young boy.

A black smoke started rising from the cabin and the third warrior came back with a long-haired scalp of brown hair. In the span of less than five minutes we had killed and scalped a family of four and had started the cabin burning.

We gathered the useful weapons. Two nice rifles and three horns of powder. Five knives and a couple axes.

Smoke was rising above the whole valley and now we could hear sporadic firing from the Cookman blockhouse. My party of warrior headed that way.

When we arrived Chiksika and Blue Jacket briefed is what had happened so far. A total of four cabins burnt. Fourteen settlers killed and scalped. 10 rifles captured. 8 horses taken. The Cookman house was the only one that could not be surprised and was putting up a resistance.

Chiksika said a young man of around seventeen, an old man and three women were in the block house. They were putting down a fierce fire. Every time a warrior would break through to the wall, boiling water would be poured down at them from the blockhouse overhang. Chiksika started launching fire arrows. The arrow tip would be wrapped in cloth and soaked in bear grease. After about twenty different arrows the roof was burning. We tried approaching the house again and the crack of a rifle dropped one of our braves with rifle ball to his forehead.

The fire started to consume the whole roof as screams started coming from the blockhouse. Not long after the first screams the door flew open and the old man came out with a pistol and a tomahawk, Blue Jacket rushed him taking a glancing blow from a pistol ball to the shoulder. Blue Jacket had the old man down and cut his throat with his large scalping knife. As the women and young boy came out they were met with the same fate of falling to knives and tomahawks.

We regrouped at our camp with our new horses. Injuries were evaluated and treated with the worst being Blue Jackets graze wound on his left shoulder. We had killed eighteen and lost one young warrior.

We ate well that night of slaughtered beef and some of the warriors had found a small barrel of rum and were making fools of themselves.

The next morning a scout came in and told us that another war party lead by Simon Girty was approaching. When they rode up, Simon briefed us on his expedition around Fort Lee (Charleston) and up the Elk River to Kenton's Bottoms and the area around Clendenin's cabin. They had surprised Fort Lee and had killed two men there. The Fort was to strong to try to sustain a siege so Girty and the warriors decided to attack and pillage the Elk River Valley and try to catch up with our party before we headed up the Elk and towards the Buckhannon River valley.

Girty's party had killed nine and burnt three cabins to the ground and had captured as many horses as we did. They had lost no braves and had only a brave with a broken leg when he fell from a cabin roof. The expedition so far was a success.

The next morning, we loaded up and headed out. We rode north on well-known Indian trails. We dropped into Little Otter country (just outside of Gassaway) and destroyed two cabins there and killing five more settlers. We crossed two mountains and dropped into the Little Kanawha River valley, here we encountered a new grouping of cabins sitting on the old town of Chief Bull of the Delawares. The Chiefs old town sat where two salt springs entered the Little Kanawha River. Him and few family members had been massacred here just a few short years ago. (Bulltown)

We broke up and used the same tactic as we did on the Big Sandy Creek and Roger's Fork. We attacked the cabins simultaneously and we killed another nine settlers and left these burning. We also found over five hundred pounds of salt bagged up in a barn. We loaded it and the pots, pans, rifles and some sacks of meal on five additional horses that we captured. We rode up the Little Kanawha and crossed a mountain making a camp above the French Creek of the Buckhannon.

The next morning, we rode on towards Bush's Fort. We arrived to find the Fort under siege by Buckhongehalas and his warriors. They had set upon the Fort a week prior to our arrival and so far had only killed one settler and had lost three braves. The disturbing thing was that a runner had escaped the fort and had ran downstream to Turkey Run and then ran up that stream. It was found out that he had made his way to the Fort on Hackers Creek. Jesse Hughes was gathering a group of men to come to the aide of Bush's.

Buckhongehalas, Chiksika and Blue Jacket held a short council. It was decided that we would keep up with a sporadic firing to save powder and lead for the next two hours. Then we would back off and half would ready the horses to leave while the other half would lay in wait to see if those in the Fort would let their guard down and open the gates thinking we had left.

We tried this. I was along the banks of the Buckhannon when there was a commotion and firing from our camp! I rolled over and headed that way. I could see a skirmish happening in the glade in front of me. I picked a target and pulled the trigger and then ran into a large white man. He swung wide with his tomahawk and it missed, I gave him the butt of my rifle to his nose.

It was then that I realized I was cut off! I had to either circle this melee or just make my way around and to the Ohio villages on my own.

Buckhongehalas had already pulled most of our group out and had started them out of the area. Jesse Hughes and his men had become distracted with me coming up behind them and had started to concentrate their firing on my position.

I bided my time and when I thought the most rifles were unloaded I jumped up and ran. Several lead balls smashed into trees around me but fortunately none hit me. I noticed in the settler's blood lust that they were going to follow me away from the Fort, this would allow my brothers to escape.

I engaged in a running battle until dark settled in. I dare not stop with about a dozen men after me. If they caught me it's hard to tell what they would do to me since I am white and carrying scalps of white men. I crossed country that I had never been in before, by daylight I had dropped into another river valley. It had to the Middle Fork. My Uncle Chancy had told me about his hunting camp in this area.

About noon I circled and came up on a rock where I could watch my back trail. It wasn't an hour until nine men slightly spread out were coming along my trail. Old Jesse Hughes was leading them. I just knew for sure I didn't want to be caught by him. The whole frontier knew he was lunatic. He could be fine one second and go off the next over nothing. Even his friends were wary of him. He was a cruel man to Indians also. He had been implicated in several murders of our hunters.

They passed on out of sight. I hurriedly gathered my things and headed out. I reasoned that if the best fighters of Hackers Creek were on my trail then that's the way I needed to go was right to Hackers Creek and hit the West Fork River and with luck find a canoe and escape that way.

I covered miles that afternoon. Crossing back into the Buckhannon River valley. Crossing over the mountain just above Bush's Fort. That evening as the twilight was setting in I hit a stream in a deep cutout canyon that was flowing towards the West Fork. (Stonecoal Creek) I made a camp here, tucked up under a massive fallen oak up against the root wall. I braved a small fire and made myself a simple gruel with some jerky, hickory nut flour and some fresh ramps as this canyon was covered in them.

The next morning, I continued down this stream for approximately eight miles then I hit the West Fork River. Here I had to make my choice. Continue down the West Fork hoping for a canoe or just cut straight overland and due west to the Ohio River. The West Fork River would have several settlements on it and most of them by now would be alarmed and warned about our attacks and would be shooting Indians on sight or I could go through some rugged country, hoping to completely lose my pursuers in the process. I decided to go due West.

I crossed the West Fork and headed up out of the valley. I hit a ridge trail that was taking me in the direction I needed to go. I made a camp that night under a rhododendron bush with no fire. Daylight brought voices close by. I awakened with a start from a dead sleep but kept my senses about laying still hidden as I was. There, not fifty yards away was Jesse Hughes and two other men sitting by a fire, roasting a deer haunch.

I could hear them talking plainly as it was a still morning. "I reckon he's heading straight fer them Ohio lands, we got to be on top of him now. I don't think he is more than three hours ahead of us. He's a white booger alright, I do not know if it's Girty or Rogers. Could be that cussed Blue Jacket, but he looks more Indian that the other two. We need catch us a white bastard to take back to the settlements and have fun with and let people get their due!"

I decided that as soon as they set their rifles down and were eating on that haunch I was making another run for it. Then another idea struck

76

me. I slid from my hiding spot and crept through the morning fog over towards them. I was behind a large chestnut tree and I checked my priming. I stood silently and came from behind that tree with my rifle cocked and the business end in their faces.

You talk about a confused crowd. Here I was standing in their camp, their rifles laying just out of their reach. "Fellows, as much as I want to kill you I am not going to discharge my rifle into one of you, if you listen. Load that haunch up in that canvass sack and Jesse, you move real slow and pick each rifle up one by one and pour the priming out. "

Now old Jesse might be off his rocker, but he wasn't stupid. He picked those rifle up real slow and did as I said. With the rifles leaning against a tree, I had them throw their knives and tomahawks over to me. I slid them down in that sack with that deer haunch. They had a pot a boiling up some tea and I took that while I gave them a speech about killing the red man and running him out of the Middle Ground. I then took my tomahawk and smashed the flints and locks as best I could on their rifles.

I took some rawhide thongs I carried in my haversack and tossed them to the short fellow. I had him tie Jesse up real good and the other fellow. Then I tied him up. I checked the binding for tightness, I took their possibles and powder horns grabbed that sack with a deer haunch in it and headed out.

I knew if I would have gone in there firing that one on three was not good odds. Figured they would think twice about trailing me on into Ohio with smashed rifles, no powder and no weapons of any kind.

I headed out and when I had put a good ten miles behind me I circled to watch my back trail. I ate half of that old deer haunch and leaned back in the sun. Confident I was not being followed I headed out on a straight line as best I could due west.

Two days later I crossed the Ohio and made course for Chillicothe. Three days after crossing the Ohio I walked into the village. The rest of the party had arrived four days before me. I hunted down Alexander McKee and gave him my notes. He thanked me for my service and gave me a small finely engraved .40 caliber pistol. I shook hands and went to find my adopted family.

The dinner fire was a happy time that evening. I had returned. Other parties were returning with prisoners, horses and captured rifles, powder and lead. Chiksika was telling his younger brother Tecumseh about the raids and the exploits of some of us "white" Indians. Deep in my mind however was this feeling, would we ever reclaim the Middle Ground?........

Chapter 12
THE STRANGE STORY OF WILLIAM STRANGE

My name is William Strange and I have spent my early years here at Fort Pitt. My Father was a British soldier stationed here but was recalled east during the revolution, he left my mother behind here but at least he had sent a monthly stipend for my schooling. I am not like the other boys my age. I really don't care for the outdoors. I prefer to keep my myself in my books and learning.

One day, Colonel Brooks called me into his office at the fort. The Colonel is in the regular United States Army. He had taken a fancy to my mother and was concerned that I had not yet picked an occupation. "William, you are 17, it is time for you to decide what you will do with yourself. You are good in mathematics and I believe surveying would be a good field for you."

"There are two surveyors here, John Hacker and Michael Cresap, they are putting a party together to head south into the interior of western Virginia to complete a survey on the upper reaches of the Elk and the Holly River. I have signed you into their crew as an apprentice and a cook."

I knew arguing would be futile. Everyone around the Fort had been calling me professor. The other boys my age would make fun of me. Many of them had been on several hunting and trapping trips down into the middle ground. Some of them had actually been in scrapes with the Shawnees, a couple even sported Indian scalps on their possible bags.

I could care less about all of that. I had been brought up in a world of books and plays. In fact I hated the dark and was scared to death of Indians. The very sight of them here at the Fort sent cold chills up and down my spine. I was just glad that the middle ground had been tamed of wild Indians somewhat.

Colonel Brooks made sure I had a good British musket. It was a .69 caliber. I had never fired one before and didn't know much about them. I put my outfit together. Wool brown knee breeches, a white shirt with a brown wool vest over it. A brown over coat of wool and a tricorn beaver felt hat. I had a green woolen blanket cape. I wore black leather boots. I have a simple sheath knife; a bark tanned deer hide bag. A horn of powder and a canvass haversack hang off my other shoulder.

I meet up with Cresap and Hacker at the warf. They have their gear and surveying tools packed. The other two look like trouble. One is a

Frenchman named Tousaint and the other is cranky smelly old man name Smith. We load in canoes and head up the Monongahela.

I have been told in no uncertain terms that I am an apprentice and the cook, nothing else. It is fine with me. I have never hunted, and I hate the wilderness. In fact, I have hardly ever fired a musket.

The nights are the worse sleeping on the cold ground. Eating half cooked meat with bare hands. The constant crudeness of my companions.

Smith keeps making advances at me calling me an Anne. I am starting to hate these bastards even before we leave the valley of this river. My own fear of Indians and the forest is what keeps me from abandoning these men.

We leave the Monongahela river and head up the West Fork and for days we head upstream through some beautiful scenery. It takes eleven days after we pass Prickett's Fort to reach the head of this West Fork river.

From there we stash the canoe for the return trip and load everything in haversacks on our back. We cut overland and cross three good size mountains to the Holly River. From there we go three days downstream and we hit the Elk River. Here we set our base camp.

My first day out with the crew I am clumsy and clueless. I mess the chain up many times and bump the compass twice. From that day on I am ridiculed and left in camp.

Every night Smith would tell Indian stories of scalping and murder and I would not sleep. The sleepless nights wore on me. The constant ridicule was maddening in my mind. The only friend I had was Cresap's hound dog he had brought on this trip.

The constant teasing the constant Indian stories were bringing me down, I couldn't eat my own cooking, after about ten days of not eating I was very weak and sick.

On the Sunday of the third week I was hunched over the fire with old hound Pete beside my feet. I stirred a pot of Bergoo when a shot was fired, and a scream of Indians was yelled from the mountain. I grabbed my musket and my possible bag with horn and ran. Pete followed me. I ran with an unimaginable fear! I don't know how far I covered but I ran until the darkness settled in four hours later. Unbeknownst to me, Touisant and Smith was laughing away in camp about how hard I ran and how far, Cresap and Hacker was saying good riddance if I didn't come back. Cresap only missed his dog Pete.

That night was cold with no blankets and not eating well the last several days, I shivered hard all night only gaining some warmth from the old hound when he laid up against me. I never thought daylight would get there soon enough. Even the daylight brought no relief immediately.

I thought I should circle the camp and check for Indians and return. I started walking. I sure was hungry. I had not thought much about food when I had it around me all the time but now I was very hungry.

I kept walking towards where I thought the camp was at. I walked all day and never got back. How far did I run? I curled up for another cold night. I woke up shivering hard no warmth came to me that day even as I covered more miles. That old hound stayed with me. He never left or wandered. A couple times he took the lead and I followed hoping to see the camp.

I had to kill something with my musket to eat. At first, I was afraid to fire, now I was into my fifth day being away from the camp. Putting one foot in front of another.

That day I came to a deep creek. I had crossed a creek several times but not one this deep. Was this the Holly River? As I tried crossing I fell hard and went over my head. I washed several yards before gaining my feet. My horn was gone! My powder wet in my rifle! I had no way to shoot, no way to hunt!

I was going on 20 days since I ate a real meal. I walked more to try for warmth. That night I shivered even harder than before. I woke up to my fingers being blue. I got up and trudged on. I flipped a rock as I stumbled and there was a millipede of some kind. I quickly dropped into my knees and grabbed him. I bit him in half and tried to chew, the texture and flavor made me wretch right away. I could not try to eat any more insects. It was too cold for lizards and snakes. I kept walking.

I don't know how many streams and miles I covered. That old hound just plodded with me getting as lank as me.

Another seven days of cold and wandering and I was gaunt. My belt didn't hold my pants, so I got rid of them. My right boot fell apart and I continued. My foot bloodied up bad. That night two of my teeth fell out.

The next day I could barely walk. I stumbled on as my right foot turned to bloody meat. That hound just followed.

That night I sneezed, and another tooth fell on the ground. The next morning, I crawled. There was another creek. I could not cross another cold stream. I could not.

I crawled downstream. My legs became as bad as my foot. My knees looked like something hanging in the Fort Pitt butcher shop.

I laid on the ground that night. The dog whimpering. Me just thinking about reading books again. If I could just find that Elk River maybe someone would pass in a canoe or a hunting party would come along.

The next day was forty-five since I had fled camp. I had no energy. I crawled twenty feet and laid against a huge sycamore. I could eat the dog! It had never occurred to me before. I had a knife and would just kill him and eat him raw until I had strength to go on. Funny thing Pete was having none of it. He knew what I was about. My legs had turned black with puss oozing out. No food and I knew I was done. I do not know why I did not think of the hound earlier.

The next morning found me unable to move from that sycamore. The hound stayed off several yards. Around noon I found strength to stand up and carve in the tree. I laid back down and could feel my lungs filling with fluid.

The next morning it took my strength to sit against the tree. A putrid blood was flowing from my nose. The last of my teeth fell out. Fifty days and no food. I leaned against the tree and closed my eyes. That night the hound curled up beside me, but I didn't know it. I was dead.

Several years passed and two hunters came upon a huge sycamore by the banks of Turkey Creek. There was a human skeleton leaning against the tree with a dog skeleton in his lap. There was a smooth bore musket and remnants of a possible bag. The year was 1835, forty years later. The bag had balls and shot but no powder horn or flask. Several fish hooks were in a tin and string. A knife was stuck in the tree with a carving. The carving said:

Strange is my Name
I be on Strange Ground
And Strange it is I won't be Found

To this day Turkey Creek has been known as Strange Creek

Chapter 13
MAD ANNE'S POWDER RUN

Fort Lee had just been finished. Replacing an old blockhouse and cabin belonging to the Clendenin family that had survived many Shawnee attacks since the early days of the revolution. Colonel George Clendenin has marched his men from Lewisburg to this site where his relatives home had stood for years and commenced to build this fort on the Great Kanawha River and the mouth of the Elk. Two of the most important waterways in the Middle Ground.

Great Britain had been defeated and the thirteen colonies had won their Independence. This did not stop the British in Detroit from still paying the Shawnee and many other tribes in Ohio country to continue their border warfare with the settlers. Kentucky was taking most of the brunt of the brutal attacks but the Shawnee, Mingos and Delawares still had not given up on the Middle Ground, even though thousands of new white settlers were pouring into the river valleys. The land of the Middle Ground was also being divided up to the Continental soldiers that had served in the Revolution. A time of great change had come to these mountains. The tide had turned, the natives could only make small in-roads with their guerrilla tactics, they could only terrorize. The Middle Ground had been lost. - - - - - -

I lost my husband to those murdering savages at the Battle of Point Pleasant. Richard Trotter treated me kind and bought out my indenture. I came to Virginia from England as a servant, but you might as well called me a slave. My name is Anne, everyone calls me Mad Anne because when my Richard was killed I took up Indian hunting as a revenge for his life.

I enjoyed wearing his old clothing. His hunting frock of butternut color, his extra tricorn surveyors hat. I carried a Good Pennsylvania long rifle built up near Lancaster. It's maple stock heavy enough to balance such a fine weapon. It is in .50 caliber. I always enjoy seeing the terror in the Red Devils eyes when they realize they are being killed by a woman.

I carry a bark tanned deer skin possible bag, a good nine-inch-long butcher knife, a plain old belt hatchet and a Tuskarawa war club out of North Carolina, passed down through my husband's family. This club with a polished granite stone inset into the hickory is my favorite method of dispatching them heathens.

I have guided settlers up and down the length of this Great Kanawha river. It sure does not take long for the men of each party to realize who the hunter, scout and boss of the party is. I can outshoot them all and I can definitely out drink them. Rum is like water to me.

1785 I remarried a good old boy named John Bailey. He is a soldier and from the Greenbrier Country. We both hunt and scout for the army and local towns. In 1788 he marched down with old Clendenin and helped build Fort Lee. It was situate where the old Clendenin block house was at on the banks overlooking the mouth of the Elk and the Kanawha. A good strong Fort here for the new country that was forming up.

1790 has been a reasonable quiet year. Indians hadn't attacked much at all in this western Virginia area. In fact, it had been my wedding year since I had even killed a red booger. I had parted his hair with that old war club while he was begging for his life, poor old guy, looked to be a century old. We were at Fort Lee hunting for the army, Old Clendenin had made some pushes up the Elk recently as rumors of war parties had made it down our way.

It was one of those lazy summer days when a person just wants to sit around and that's just what I was doing. Leaning back against an outer wall asleep when a yell woke me. A soldier was stumbling through the gate all bloody. He was yelling, "Indians!". You know we got that gate closed just in time. At least twenty-five came up off the Kanawha River Bank and at the front of the Fort. I fired through the gate a killing one. One of the young soldier boys manning the gate fell with half his skull missing. I ran and put my shoulder to the gate just as those heathens hit the gate. We dropped the cross bar in place. I then ran up on the cat walk and started looking for targets.

I reloaded and sighted on a leg sticking out from behind a log. I fired, and that red devil screamed. That's one that would not be rushing our Fort. The other men began laying down a fire and repulsing the Indians. They looked to be all Shawnee warriors. Oh, how I wanted to be amongst them with my war club bashing their brains!

The torrid pace of fire kept up through the afternoon. We had plenty of food and water. Lead was no problem, but powder was a different story. Just a short week ago Colonel Clendenin had been ordered to send four barrels of powder to Fort Randolph at Point Pleasant. More and more Shawnee's had been attacking flat boats on the Ohio and it was figured the attack would happen on that Fort.

By evening another fifteen canoes of warriors had come down the Elk and had started to take part in the siege. Colonel Clendenin ordered us to only fire if the target presented a sure kill. The daylight faded into a hazy dusk and that's when the barrage of fire arrows began flying over the walls. We were kept busy a stomping fires while trying to man our post. One arrow did a good job of starting the arsenal cabin to burning. The men were fighting desperately to put the fire out but to no avail, with in ten minutes our last forty-pound keg of powder went up in an explosion that weakened the section of the wall. We all were down to what we had in our powder horns and flasks.

Colonel Clendenin called a general council of his officers. It was decided that someone needed to try a powder run to Fort Randolph. I volunteered.

This being cooped up inside this Fort was not for me. If I had to die at least let me be under the trees a fighting for my life. My sweet John tried talking me out of it but finally relented. I was a going.

That night I readied all my possibles. I slipped out the hole created by the powder explosion and made my way towards the Elk River. If I could get a canoe I could be at Fort Randolph by noon tomorrow. I slipped quietly along the river bank. I saw a form in the fog that didn't look right so I slid towards it silently. It was a sentry and I quickly hit him with my war club full force in the back of the skull. He would not be shooting at any forts again. The canoes were closely watched. To many warriors were camped around them. I went quietly around them to the Kanawha bank. I stuck my knife into the ribs of another sentry and let him bleed out before I released my grip from over his mouth. This side was just as bad, at least forty warriors were wrapping cloth around arrows and talking quietly.

I backed off and did some thinking. If I headed to Fort Randolph, I would be heading right for Shawnee territory and who was to say that Fort Randolph was not under siege also. I could go up the river to the Greenbrier country to Fort Savannah at Lewisburg. This trip would be over a hundred miles of rugged terrain, but I would not be heading right into the Shawnee nation. It did not take me long to decide and I took off.

I tried in the dark to hide my trail, knowing that as soon as the two dead sentries were discovered that I would be followed. I ran on up the trail. I crossed Campbell's Creek and Witcher Creek before the sun started to rise. I was covering ground but doubling back every once in a while, to check my back trail.

The third time that day I doubled back and sure enough here come six of the Red Devils on my trail. I dropped in behind them and ghosted them until they found my cut back trail. I then lit on out of there. I ate biscuits from the Fort. I was hoping to get distance on the Shawnee so I could kill a deer and eat some good meat but that was not going to happen, and I would have to just make do. I took off again and hoped to put some distance between us.

I ghosted on through the big timber on the banks of Great Kanawha. I was nearing the falls near where the Gauley dumps in. I wanted to somehow get behind those six and start a hunting them, I was tired of being the hunted. As I started to hear the roar of the falls I came upon a large Sycamore that had a two foot by three-foot opening in the base. As a light drizzle had just started I crawled in. It was just in time, as the clouds opened and a hard downpour started. I situated myself until I could get a shot out the opening if need be. It was at that moment I heard the buzzing behind me. I carefully drew my knife and turned my head. There was a timber rattler about 4 feet long curled by my left ankle.

I slowly rolled and sat up. I could see the rascals head and as quick as a whip I grabbed him behind his cussed head. A quick swipe later and I had a writhing bit of dinner in my hands. I peeled his skin back and started gnawing on him raw. It was meat and it was good. A little bloody but I needed it.

As I was a chewing on that old snake here come those six braves right down the river bank.

They were confused, they had lost my trail. They were working up the bank combing every inch looking for some trace of my passing. After they passed on, I fell asleep. I was tired after the trail and slept the sleep of the dead.

After about eight hours of good sleep I started in behind those scoundrels. I crept forward all day. I crossed the Gauley and hit the old midland trail that ran the length of the New River into the mountains on the North Carolina border. Those braves had figured that I was heading to Fort Savannah and I picked up their sign on the trail.

That night I saw their fire out ahead of me. They were camped on a chestnut flat right off the trail. They were not even trying to hide their fire. I crept right up to their sentry and silently put my hand over his mouth and pulled him to the ground. I slit his throat with my scalper. After his blood had watered the ground and his struggles ceased I let him go. I checked my priming and cocked my rifle. I pulled my war club and readied myself.

I took off on a dead run and let go with a mighty scream such as my great grandfather would have let loosed in the Scotch Highlands at his enemies. Those five sat right up! My rifle cracked in the chest of the closest warrior and my war club swung and made a bloody mist of another's brain.

The last three were so stunned that I didn't hear them a yipping and, on my trail, until I put a good five hundred yards on them.

I had cut their force by half in about a two-minute span and they were angry. I left the midland trail about ten miles further along and cut up a mountain. I crossed a mountain meadow and then circled back on my trail. I laid amongst some rocks and cocked my rifle.

Those three braves came creeping out into that meadow at over a hundred paces. I leveled off on the back one and gave a little elevation. I set my back trigger and squeezed slightly on the front one. The rifle jumped in my hands. The brave crumpled.

I was off on a dead run out of there while the other two were arguing from a hiding spot on what they should do.

After about six hours of hard running I collapsed at a spring. I drank long and deep and noticed there were tadpoles in the spring. I caught some in my hand and started eating them. I was feeling starved but just knew I didn't have no space to hunt.

I took off again and ran. I had to get to that fort on the morrow for sure. That night I curled up along a log and tried to sleep for an hour.

I woke with a start looking into the barrel of a gun. The brave turned his head and yelled a slur about me. While his head was turned I stabbed him quickly in the thigh and knocked him down. I slammed my war club on his shoulder crushing it then stuck my knife between his ribs into his heart. I grabbed my things and ran into the dark.

I ran like a deer that day covering the ground. Crossing stream after stream, mountain after mountain. The last warrior was running also, it seemed he stayed at about three hundred yards the whole day. That evening I dropped into the valley and within sight of Fort Savannah.

The brave had closed to about a hundred yards when he up and fired his rifle at me. The ball grazed the left side of my head and sent me tumbling. I got up dazed and bloody.

That brave was bearing down on me with his tomahawk and knife drawn. I drew my knife and war club. He swung his hawk and I met it with my club. They locked. I stabbed upwards hard with my knife and drove it deep into his chest while he looked into my eyes. As he fell to the ground three militia men from the fort met me as I fell to the ground.

"By gosh Captain it's a woman!" That was all I heard the young private yell, then I fainted. I woke up in the Fort with General Andrew Lewis himself looking down on me. I explained to him about Fort Lee and the siege. He looked at me skeptically when I explained to him that the warrior I had killed in front of the gate earlier was the last of six, that I had killed all the others on my trail.

The General said he couldn't spare a man but that he would give me two horses and two forty-pound kegs of powder. I got up out of that bed and readied myself. With the powder they gave me a good bait of food too.

I took those horses off on a trot. It had taken five whole days to cover hundred plus miles to Fort Savannah. It only took me two whole days of hard riding to get within sight of Fort Lee. I could not see any better way than to just take those two horses on a dead run right at the gate and hope that those gents inside covered me and let me in safely. I tied my rifle off on the saddle and put wrist through the thong of my war club.

I started the horses on a run from about a mile out and let loose with my war scream.

A brave came from hiding and I ran him down with my horse. Another reached and grabbed my leg and I smashed him with my club. As I closed in within a hundred yards the forts rifle starting cracking. I was fairly surrounded by warriors. I kept swinging the club, maiming and killing braves as best I could. I swept through the open gate with one brave being drug in by the pack horse. He immediately was shot down by about six soldiers!

I slumped from the horse into John's arms. A huzzah went up from the fort's soldiers! I had done it. I had covered two hundred plus miles in seven days. I had killed eleven Red Devils for sure and injured who knows how many. My cross-country trip had saved these men and also insured the strangle hold by the whites on this Middle Ground.

Chapter 14
CAPTAIN JEREMIAH ROGERS,
HIS MAJESTIES ROYAL ARMY

I had just returned from raids deep into the Middle Ground of Western Virginia. I had turned a well-kept journal of what I had seen and the strength of the western frontier to Alexander McKee.

I returned to my lodge and laid back on my bedding. It had been a long month of riding and fighting. Would I ever get to return to my small claimed homestead on Roger's Fork on Big Sandy Creek?

1777 found the frontier in chaos. Many of my Red brothers had been murdered which had caused a bloody war on the settlers that committed the atrocities. The war in the east is raging between the British and the Colonials. The British have taken to paying the Shawnee and all the northwest tribes for scalps and prisoners. Governor Henry Hamilton has been pushing for more attacks and has filled the Indian villages with trade muskets, gun powder, lead, tomahawks and red handled scalping knives.

This war is the last great chance to push settlements back across the Alleghenies. The Virginians already had a strong foothold on the Ohio. Fort Pitt and Pittsburgh was a large town and very established. Fort Henry at Wheeling was still vulnerable, and an attack was being planned their by the Wyandots.

Further down the Ohio, Fort Randolph has been built on the site of the Battle of Point Pleasant. This point of land stuck out into the water where the great Kanawha empties into the Ohio. Soon a plan would be made to attack this fort also.

The task ahead of the Northwest tribes was monumental and could not be accomplished without help from the British.

I, Jeremiah "Cat" Rogers was caught up in this war. I had grown up near the New River where it came from the mountains of North Carolina. I had hunted the Middle Ground with my Uncle Chancy, surviving a mauling by a panther and thus gaining my nickname.

My parents had been slaughtered by these very Shawnees and my sister captured. I had tracked them down after a year and won her back. I had become friends of the Delaware, Mingos and the Shawnee in the process. I had learned from their great chiefs and holy men about their ways and this life. I had learned of Moneto and how he had given the

91

red men all that they needed as long as they respected this Mother Earth that is so carefully balanced on the back of a great turtle. I had excepted this life and beliefs as my own. I had here my strong brothers to Chiksika and Blue Jacket. Respected for my white point of view by Cornstalk and Buckhongehalas. I had found my home.

I dozed in the warmth of my lodge. The images of war and attacks going through my head. Those soon replaced by dreams of hunting and trapping the frontier.

A "hello" brought me from my dreams. I jumped up and went out of the lodge and there was Alexander McKee. He had reviewed my journal and wanted to talk to me about it. I had included several drawings of the many forts and blockhouses we had passed or attacked on our last long ride.

He was impressed and wanted me to accompany him to Detroit where I could brief Governor Henry Hamilton on our latest raids and what might be needed to push the Colonial settlers back over the mountains. I immediately started to get my things together to leave at dawn.

We loaded up and rode out on the morning. I had not been much further north and west than Kispoko town. After three days of hard riding we came to Detroit. It reminded a lot of Fort Pitt. Several more Indians here however.

Alexander McKee took me to the governor's house. We were shown in and taken to a couple rooms where we could dress to meet the Governor. I had brought a pair of Doe skin pants. Over this I wore a deep blue long hunter shirt. I wore my hair pulled back into a long que. I had on a beautiful pair of quilled elkskin moccasins made by a Wyandot woman that lived near Kispoko.

When I changed I came out of the room and Alexander had changed into his British army uniform. He was an official British Major.

We were led into the Governor's office. "Major it is could to see you. Mr. Rogers it is a pleasure to meet you." With that we sat down, and Major McKee and the governor talked at depth about our last raid. I was asked several questions and tried to explain my drawings and notes to the fullest.

After a couple hours and several cups of brandy, I think the Governor had a very good grasp on what was taking place across the Ohio to the Alleghenies. Governor Hamilton rose and walked over and looked out a window overlooking the compound. "Jeremiah Rogers, I am going to commission you as a Captain in His Majesties army. You will draw a captains pay. I am going to send five pack animals with muskets, powder, lead, tomahawks and knives. I want you to put together a force and attack Fort Randolph at Point Pleasant. At the same tome Major McKee will make a thrust through Wheeling to Fort Pitt if possible. If not, he would take his force into the Monongahela River valley and will destroy as many outposts as possible there. If you cannot take the Fort you are to take your force up the Kanawha then up the Gauley, crossing into the Elk watershed. From there destroy every cabin you come across back to Ohio."

The Major saluted the Governor and we turned and left. Alexander told me to get a good night's sleep and we would leave first thing in the morning. As I was settling in there was a knock on my door. I answered and there was a Lieutenant standing there. "Sir, the Governor wished for me to measure you for uniform. "I allowed him to do what he had to do.

The next morning, we were making sure our loads on the pack animals we were given were loaded correctly when the Lieutenant approached me with a uniform in hand. I shrugged into the coat and he saluted me. I packed away the pants, shirts and boots. I wore the jacket and the gorget.

"Well Cat, you are a striking Indian in that scarlet coat." We rode out of Detroit at a fair clip. We covered the ground back to Kispoko town in three days.

As we rode into town several of the warriors and their wives came out of their lodges and pointed at me and were talking amongst themselves. We rode up to the council lodge and unloaded the horses. McKee went and talked to Blue Jacket and Chiksika about a general council to give the goods away and to come up with a plan to strike into the Middle Ground.

Runners were sent out to the other Shawnee towns. Also, to the Miamis, Wyandots, Delawares, Mingos and Weas. A council was called for on the next full moon.

During that month long wait the men all hunted to put away meat for the winter ahead. I found myself hunting one day with Tecumseh, Chiksika's younger brother.

I always enjoyed spending time with him. He hunted well with his hickory bow. For a youngster he sure could draw and handle a man's bow.

We were hiding along a log watching a trail that cut up from a creek bottom onto the plain behind us. Chiksika and Blue Jacket were stalking the creek bottom and hoping to move deer in our direction. The November leaves that were left on the trees were brilliant and the smell of autumn filled the air, it was a grand time to be alive.

The sound of a stick popping brought our attention to bear on the trail. I eased the hammer back on my .40 rifle. Tecumseh's muscles tightened and then a large buck materialized on the trail in front of us. Tecumseh came to one knee, drew and released all in one fluid motion. The arrow flew and slammed the buck perfectly behind the front shoulder and low.

The buck jumped and bucked, breaking the wood shaft off and running the hard run of a mortally wounded deer. Crashing less than an arrow flight away in the prairie behind us. I let out a whoop and slapped Tecumseh on the back. Chiksika and Blue Jacket caught up to us just as we arrived at the deer. Tecumseh had made an incredible kill for a boy that was so very young.

I jogged around the creek to where we had left our horses about a mile back. I rode up and we loaded the buck across Tecumseh's horse.

As we rode back to the village two warriors were approaching us riding their horses hard! "Come quickly to the village! Our beloved Chief Cornstalk has been murdered at the white man's Fort Randolph!"

We urged our horses into a run. When we arrived back into the village many women and men were stripping down and covering their bodies with black wood ash and wailing and crying. We immediately went to the council house where the messengers were readying themselves to give the official account of what happened.

Cornstalk and Red Hawk, another Shawnee Chief, has went to the Fort to give the White men notice that the Shawnees were going to war against the frontier and there was nothing he could do to hold them back. Captain Matthew Arbuckle did not take this talk as a warning but as a direct threat from Cornstalk and since Cornstalk was here delivering the threat Arbuckle decided to hold Cornstalk and RedHawk as prisoners.

When Cornstalk did not arrive back to his canoe where his son Elinipsico was waiting to take the two chiefs back to Ohio, Elinipsico went to the Fort to check on his father. He was taken hostage also.

Not long after Elinipsico's arrival two of the Fort's hunters, Hamilton and Gilmore were discovered murdered and scalped along the Kanawha River. A mob began to form and the door to the cabin where the Shawnees were kept was being broke down. Red Hawk scrambled up the chimney to try to make an escape while Cornstalk calmed his son and encouraged him to stand and face what Moneto had in store for them.

The door burst open and the men emptied their rifles and pistols into the two them commenced to mutilate the bodies with knives and tomahawks. They then found Red Hawk in the chimney and pulled him down and killed him with their tomahawks and knives.

This ended the life of our great Chief Cornstalk, who had gone to the whites in peace to give them a warming and had been murdered for this.

The entire Shawnee nation fell into mourning.

After a week the call went out. All warriors need come to a grand council. The Shawnees are requiring the Wyandots, Delawares, Miamis, Weas, Powatomies, Mingos, Chippewas, Ottawas and Hurons to come and fight. No longer would just the Shawnee be the buffer. No longer would the Shawnee be the tribe to lose their chiefs and warriors. A great council was held at Chagawaltha.

This grand council went on for days. The planned war ahead was deeply discussed. Each chief of each tribe let their opinion be known. Alexander McKee, Simon Girty and I gave long speeches. When all speeches and oratory had ended a plan was made. Simon Girty and a group of four to five hundred Wyandots, Shawnees and other tribes would make a push through Wheeling to Dunkard Creek attacking Fort Henry and destroying homesteads in this area. I would be taking a second group to Fort Randolph and besieging it while destroying as many homesteads as we could up the Great Kanawha, the Elk, the Gauley, the New and the Greenbrier. The goal was to kill or capture every white person that was encountered.

The war dancing continued every evening for the next few days. Governor Hamilton sent another supply train with more muskets, knives, tomahawks, powder and lead.

I prepared myself. I wore deer skin leggings and a red wool breechclout. A fine dark blue long shirt out of tradecloth is what I picked to wear and topped this with my red coat. My weapons were my .40 caliber rifle that I had been through so much with. In my belt was a silver inlaid smooth bore pistol. My knife in a deerskin sheath. In my belt in the small of my back I had my pipehawk pushed down in. I carried with me everything I would need for this campaign in a deerskin possible bag, a canvass haversack and rolled up in my blue wool blanket. The two paints I carried with me to paint up for battle were a black and a pale yellow.

McKee changed our plans as we prepared to ride out. He said that Girty would go ahead and attack Fort Henry and all the settlements and cabins that he could but he wanted myself, Chiksika and Blue Jacket to head to Kentucky first on a raid, returning to the villages with prisoners before then resulting and attacking into the western Virginia frontier.

We rode out, a good four hundred strong. After two days we crossed the Ohio into Kentucky. We broke into four parties and separated. We attacked, St. Asaph, Harrold's Fort, Boones Fort and Lexington simultaneously. Sweeping from the Ohio to the Tennessee country. We burned forty-three cabins and blockhouses while killing thirty-two men and boys. We captured another twenty-four women and girls and eleven young boys. We even took seven men prisoners. It was a bloody yet necessary affair, the whites for too long had taken and pushed the Indian out of his hunting grounds.

We rode back into the Ohio villages and McKee made sure our prisoners that were not bound for the stake were delivered to Detroit.

We once again rode out heading for Point Pleasant. We crossed the Ohio and surrounded Fort Randolph. We crept in as close as we dated and at daylight the siege began. The firing was intense and continued throughout the early morning. A pale smoke arose over the grounds. When the sun reached a midday peak, me and Chiksika approached under a flag of truce. "I am Captain Jeremiah Rogers of His Majesties Army, I would like to speak with Captain Arbuckle!"

Soon someone yelled, "we are sending an emissary to you".

Nonhelema stepped out of the gate and walked over to us. We retreated well out of rifle range to speak.

"You will not take this fort without a British canon. The walls are to strong and the men are well armed, fed and determined. I come to you so that you may save Warriors. Do not rush this fort without cannon. The Captain also wishes that I tell you, he will not surrender. "

With that she walked back to the Fort and disappeared inside. The firing commenced and continued throughout the day.

Chiksika, Blue Jacket and I held a council with some of the other chiefs and warriors. It was determined to leave about one hundred fifty warriors here to continue holding the soldiers in siege. We would then break into three smaller war parties and set up the Kanawha to destroy as many homesteads as we could.

We readied ourselves and pulled out in the night. It was a cool May night and the Spring peepers were deafening in the swamps and sloughs along the Kanawha. As we approached the confluence of the Elk and Kanawha the next day it was determined that Chiksika would take a group and attack the Clendenin blockhouse, Chief Wolf Eyes of the Wyandots would take his party on up the Kanawha and attack Fort Donally on the Greenbrier. I would take a group of Shawnees, Delawares and Mingos and would make a sweep up the Elk and cross into the Little Kanawha drainage and return to the Ohio villages by that route.

We all set out. We camped that night off a Warriors trail looking down on the Elk. The group I was leading was sizeable, large enough that I had no doubt we could wipe out any cabin we came too.

The next morning, we crept into view of three cabins that had been built in an area called Kenton's Bottom. We swiftly attacked there, killing two men and boy and capturing three women and a girl. We burned those cabins.

Loading our prisoners up and we rode on. We approached where the Big Sandy Creek entered the Elk River. Here, another blockhouse cabin had been built. We quietly approached on foot after hiding the horses. There was a man and a black man working in a corn field. I sent three of the braves toward the cabin. Another warrior and I crawled and entered the corn field.

We closed the distance to mere feet when the three braves let out a whoop at the cabin. The men turned and looked at the commotion and this gave us our opportunity to strike. I had instructed the brave with me not to kill the black man but to take him prisoner and that is exactly what he did. Grabbing him and pulling him to the ground.

I, on the other hand, had a fight on my hands. The settler had a hoe in one hand and a pistol in his belt. He immediately pulled the pistol and fired it in my face. I had hit his arm just enough and felt the ball take the top of my left ear off.

I yelled in anger and tackled him. He escaped out of my grip and swung his hoe at me. I parried his blow with my tomahawk. He swung once more at me and I went under the swing and swung my tomahawk. The swing of my tomahawk hit his hand, damaging it significantly. He dropped the hoe and turned to run.

I ran him down and jumped on his back. I plunged my knife into his chest three times. As he sunk to the ground I took his scalp with a swift slice and a pull. I then sat on the ground and got my breath.

The firing had ceased, and the cabin was burning. My ear was bleeding profusely but amazingly it was not a painful wound. The other warriors had killed a woman and a small boy, they had their scalps and were elated with the success we had.

As we gathered together we made a decision to keep riding up the Elk. Just the year before we had hit the Big Sandy drainage hard, wiping out all the settlements in that area.

We rode through some of the most amazing wilderness. The valley of the Elk was a paradise full of towering sycamore and hemlock. The hillsides covered in chestnut. Game was still everywhere including the fat elk this river was known for.

We rode on. We passed tributaries that were emptying in such as the Big Otter and Strange Creek. We rode for the next two days to where the Holly empties in. Here was the old land claimed by my Uncle Chancy that had returned to wilderness since he had ventured to the Missouri River country and had not returned to the Middle Ground.

We stayed for two days here to replenish our food. Our prisoners were apprehensive, but I tried to reassure them that they would not be harmed. They would either be adopted into the tribe or taken to the British at Detroit.

After killing a couple deer and an elk. We smoked the meat and made jerky. Loading this up we headed out once again. We rode up the Holly until we hit an old trail that crossed a mountain and we dropped into the Little Kanawha valley.

We rode for three days before we reached a mountain where we were overlooking Parker's settlement. (Parkersburg)

We struck it with full force, surprising three of the men that were working fields and cutting wood. We took another small boy and girl prisoner before the firing from the blockhouses was too great to continue to risk the lives of the warriors.

We hurriedly crossing the Ohio and headed into the interior to Chalahawtha. I sent two scouts back to watch our back trail. After riding half a day one of the scout's came riding up. "We are followed by eleven men on horses. They are coming fast."

We quickly convened and came up with a plan. The trail we were on would cut through a wooded ravine in the next mile. We would hurry to get there and send two braves with the prisoners on ahead. The rest of us would lay in wait and the two rear scouts would lead the white men into our ambush.

We quickly setup and the scout returned to our back trail. We did not have long to wait as the scouts returned a little over an hour later riding hard. They galloped past us. The party of whites were only three hundred yards behind. When the last rider was approaching my position, I fired. A loud cacophony if shots followed. Nine saddles empties. We screamed and attacked. I swing my hawk and killed a man that had his arm broken by a ball at the elbow. I turned to face any other possible enemies, and all were dead but two. Those two had whirled their horses and headed back to the Ohio. We gathered horses and picked up rifles, knives and tomahawks. One of the Wyandots quickly beheaded one of the followers and stuck his scalped head on a sharpened stick by the trail as a warning to anyone else that decided to follow.

We rode on to Chalahawtha. We arrived back to find all other parties had returned. Fort Henry and Fort Randolph has with stood their sieges. With that said we had killed upwards of one hundred fifty settlers from Dunkard Creek and Catfish Camp in the north to the Greenbrier valley in the south east and the Kentucky settlements to the due south.

That night over a fire Blue Jacket, Chiksika, Tecumseh and myself talked the night away. We talked of what had been and what would be. The future was bleak. We had successes but every time a white was killed, ten came in his place. The old ways were disappearing for the Indian. My race was pushing hard and taking the Middle Ground for them self and here I am, Captain Jeremiah "Cat" Rogers, adopted Shawnee white warrior, British Captain, son of a White settler, stuck in the middle. I looked at Blue Jacket, the Girty brothers and Alexander McKee and wondered what was to become of us? Would we ever be able to return to homes we hold dear? Or would we constantly be pushed away with the Shawnee, Wyandot, Miami, Mingo and Delaware from our Middle Ground?